THROUGH THE FIRE

RAJ LOWENSTEIN

Order this book online at www.trafford.com
or email orders@trafford.com

Most Trafford titles are also available at major online book retailers.

Print information available on the last page.

ISBN: 978-1-4907-6838-0 (sc)
ISBN: 978-1-4907-6840-3 (hc)
ISBN: 978-1-4907-6839-7 (e)

Library of Congress Control Number: 2015920972

Trafford rev. 06/10/2016

www.trafford.com

North America & international
toll-free: 1 888 232 4444 (USA & Canada)
fax: 812 355 4082

DEDICATION

To all those who have supported, encouraged, and loved me although I haven't written down your names, I thank you.

I want to thank my family for helping me keep my feet on the ground while allowing me to still have my head in the clouds.

To Diane Adler and Susan Reed, thanks for the spell-check!

To Linda A. and Gail S., how about dim sum?

To Mark S., I love you and miss you. Thank you!

To "Michael," thanks for the inspiration and for letting me use a little of your life for my book.

To Dan, my brother and twin, I love you and miss you. You are always in my heart, my dreams, and my prayers. I wrote "David" for you to give you what you should have had.

To my children, Jeff, Cameron, and Chelcé, I love you all! Also, of course, to my grandkids, Bubbie loves you!

To my husband, Richard J., "El Amor de Mi Vida," who, even though he thinks I am a bit "out there," loves and supports me anyway. Because of you, all this is possible. I love you!

FOREWORD

American Sign Language, or ASL, is not English. It is a unique and beautiful language that's recognized as a language such as Spanish, French, or Swahili. It is full of rich nuances and subtleties. It is not universal. Each country has its own form of sign language or at least uses a form of a sign language that was brought to the country.

When the characters in this book use ASL, I have translated their American Sign Language into English. I want to stress, again, that if a character is discussing some concept, it might take five articulated signs to complete the thought in ASL and five or six sentences to say in English. Or conversely, a thought that can be expressed in three or four words in English might require ten articulated signs to interpret correctly into ASL.

So while it might seem as if all the characters are using English, this is just to help the story flow and keep the comprehension level on an equal footing.

Furthermore, I do not have any idea of how real police officers work. Like most Americans, fortunately or unfortunately, all my working knowledge comes for watching *Law and Order* and *CSI*. So I want to apologize in advance to any law enforcement personnel who will read this and cringe, especially to my son and daughter-in-law, who are the real deal, who will read this and cringe.

Through the Fire

Music and lyrics by David Foster, Tom Keane, Cynthia Weil
As sung by Chaka Khan

When it's this good there's no saying no
I need you so I'm ready to go
Through the fire, to the limit, to the wall
For just to be with you I'd gladly risk it all
Through the fire, through whatever come what may
For a chance at loving you, I'd take it all the way . . .
Right down to the wire, even through the fire

PROLOGUE

He crushed out another cigarette, grinding the butt into the concrete surface of the parking garage. He counted the fourteen butts, knowing that when this "little incident" was finished, there would be no trace of them to mark the more than three hours that had passed since he had taken his position in the shadows. The three hours of waiting was fine with him; he had waited for years for this opportunity. It had cost him time and money, but the Lord Jesus and his father had both told him when the Abomination had been born twenty-nine years ago, it would need to be destroyed. The Lord hadn't told him it was going to be easy or even how to dispatch the beast, but serving the Lord involved faith and belief. He had both.

He remembered the first time he had seen the Abomination. He had been eleven, the Abomination five and its brother almost eight. He had known it was what it was, yet he had felt protective toward it. It was quiet and beautiful with eyes so large and trusting it broke his heart to know what was coming.

"It is evil, a goddamned Abomination," his father's voice reverberated in his memory. "Its mother was a whore, and its father was a lover of Satan. Why else would it be what it is, have the eyes of evil? Even"—his father's voiced pitched as if delivering one of his Sunday sermons—"the silence is not natural, it's against God."

Catfish hadn't understood what his father had meant at that time. All he could see was the tear-filled eyes of an innocent child, but the devil often appeared in the guise of the innocent. Catfish understood that now. His whole life began to change that night in the basement of his northern Georgia farmhouse.

He had never understood how the two strange children had been deposited on his father's doorstep. Oh, Catfish—that was what he had been called—knew the genealogy and the circumstances, but somewhere he remembered thinking, for a brief span of time, they had been safe from what he had lived with his entire short life.

That night, the night when the boy had been tied up so he could watch the Abomination receive what it had coming, with a thin cane of bamboo, Catfish had whipped the Abomination until its silent screams had become too loud. Each thwack of the cane against flesh still echoed in his ears.

However, now it had become the sound of erotic pleasure, and before this night was over, he would hear it again.

As he waited in the garage, his father's voice came to him again. "Do you see it? It is a sign." His father assured him with a hint of fanaticism in his harsh voice, pointing at the Abomination's astonishing eyes. "They are the first." Then with rising excitement, his father indicated the Abomination's unnatural silence as the second sign before finally indicating the third. "Look at it!" He had yelled before spitting in the face of the five-year-old. Catfish had looked at it, and his cock became so hard it had hurt.

Catfish remembered his father smiling as he reached down to cup his crotch. "Now you understand why it must be killed. But first, it must suffer. The Lord Jesus will tell you what to do."

There had been two days of beatings for the Abomination before the vile monster's brother had freed himself and found help. When the local sheriff showed up at the house behind the Word of the Holy Book Evangelical Church, the house of Pastor Buford Carl Mosby, at three in the morning, they discovered the naked, exhausted, hungry, and filthy boy had not been lying. The children had been whisked away to the hospital in Murphy, Georgia, until their mother had been located, and Catfish had been placed in protective custody.

Later, Catfish would learn that the two children's maternal grandparents, wealthy doctors from Dublin, Ireland, had been contacted and took them back, along with their mother, to the land of silkies, fairies, and other creatures of Satan.

Catfish's father had not survived the scandals that followed, but he had. He had leaned many things from his father; among the diversity of them all was how to be a good liar. His father had suffered, been denigrated, and humiliated, and he planned on doing the same thing to the Abomination.

He had located it once he had turned twenty-three, and while it still lived in Ireland but returned to the states for its father's funeral, he hadn't succeeded in killing it, only in making it suffer. He had enjoyed that, making it suffer. He found pleasure in someone else's pain. The Abomination's brother and others had stopped him before he could rid the world of this creature. But he had left marks on top of those he had placed before to show the world on the outside what ugliness was on the inside.

The sound of the elevator brought Catfish back to the present. Before he stepped back into the shadow to wait, he glanced at his watch: 8:46 p.m.

The sound of footsteps on the concrete quickened his heart. He waited, silent and still. A man's deep voice called out, and the sound of the shoes stopped.

He knew its schedule. His man, who would clean up any traces of his presence, had followed and recorded its every movement for the month since he had discovered where it had been hiding itself. Monday was the day it left the office late. For twelve years, he had waited for a third chance to rid the earth of this Abomination; he could wait a few more minutes. The fact that it was Halloween made this even better; he could take out the devil on its own satanic holiday.

"Okay," the man's voice said from the direction of the elevator, "I'll see you tomorrow." The sound of the elevator doors closing echoed throughout the canyon of parked cars.

There it was. It had stepped out of the protected cover of the elevators and was heading to its car. Catfish waited. The car would not start; he had made sure of that. It would get into its car, and when the sleek convertible wouldn't start, it would notice the hood ajar, just enough for it to get out and see what the reason was.

A smile pulled his unnaturally thin lips tight. He wasn't going to kill it, he had decided, not yet. First it would suffer. Oh, yes. The world would know it was an Abomination before he sent it straight to hell.

He watched it get out and gazed at the hood.

Catfish moved quickly, quietly.

Later, as Catfish and his associate pulled out of the parking garage, he pulled a disposable phone from the glove box of the utility van and hit redial. On West Cottage Street in the Heights, a small 1920s Craftsmen Style bungalow was engulfed by flames.

"Well, now," Catfish said to the man driving, "did you find what I was looking for? The younger, the better, but legal."

The man driving was uncomfortable and a little afraid of him, and he liked that. Fear often made things better. "Yes, sir, they're waiting."

"Good. Now, let the fun continue!"

Michael became aware of voices. They were faint, not real. Pain began to make its presence known. It was subtle, but as the voices became clearer, the pain became more focused.

Light seeped under Michael's eyelids, burning through. The light added to the pain.

Michael tried to move.

"Doctor," a voice to Michael's left said.

"Michael." Another voice, a different woman, spoke. "If you can understand me, squeeze your left hand."

Michael concentrated on squeezing but wasn't sure if the connection from brain to hand was working.

"Doctor, Michael's coming around," the voice, a third, said.

"Michael, you're at St. Luke's. I called Dr. Hartman and told him we had you. He wanted to come, but I told him to let you rest. Do you remember what happened?" the voice asked.

Michael squeezed the nurse's hand several times.

"Once for yes, twice for no," the voice said.

"No," the nurse's voice interpreted.

"Okay, don't worry about that now. I know you're in pain, and we're going to give you something now. I needed to wait until after the x-rays were read. You have no serious injuries, as far as we can tell, but you were worked over pretty good." The voices began to fade.

Michael didn't fight the slipping away. Michael hurt from head to toe. The last thought was of remembering somewhere, deep down, the word "Abomination," but it, like consciousness, faded away.

CHAPTER 1

Dr. David Hartman stood at the nurse's station outside room 613. He had told Dr. Collin Smith, the ER attending the night before, he had wanted Michael to have a private room. He would see that the costs were taken care of. Michael was not only an employee of his medical practice but a close friend. David had already called Michael's brother, Sean, to let him know the situation. David had assured Sean Michael would be okay and there was no need for him to fly in from Seattle to Houston. He had promised once Michael was settled and a few days had passed, David would make sure Michael called and checked in.

He scanned the chart. Whoever had attacked Michael had been angry. The police officers had said they see this kind of violence when it is personal, a crime of passion. Michael's hair had been chopped off with some kind of shears, then later, had been shaved in the ER so the crescent-shaped laceration on the left side of Michael's head could be sutured together.

Some sort of chemical spray had been sprayed into Michael's face, into the eyes. The ophthalmologist on staff didn't think there would be any lasting damage, but those beautiful eyes would have to be irrigated every few hours and kept covered for the next week.

What had shocked David the most was the report of the scars on Michael's back, from shoulders to buttocks. Most were old wounds, Smith had said, most likely from a cane or whip of some type. There were a few newer lacerations, but they were on top of the older ones.

It had occurred to David that even though they lived in the hot humidity of Houston, Texas, he had never once seen Michael without a shirt in the full light of day. Even when they had put each other to bed after a night of heavy college drinking, Michael had seen David naked, but it occurred to him, he had never seen Michael's back when there would have been enough light to have noticed the heavy scarring. He had known Michael for almost twelve years and had no idea Michael had been abused in such a sick manner.

In addition to the lacerations, there was a broken nose, busted lip, and bruises that started at Michael's shins and traveled up to beneath the ears. The broken nose and lacerations had been tended to by the plastic surgeon on staff; everything else would need time to heal.

David took a deep breath and opened the door to the private room. Like most of the private rooms, it was furnished with a sofa bed, table, and chairs arranged in a sitting room. In the center of the room against the wall was a cleverly disguised hospital bed, and on the bed was Michael.

David glanced at his Rolex; it was ten in the morning. Michael had been admitted at eleven the night before, so David was confident that Michael was not asleep. The movement of the gauze-covered head proved David correct.

"You could have asked me for a week off if you needed to have a vacation." The sound of his rich voice was hollow even to his ears. This was why doctors didn't treat family, and Michael was family. There was not a sound from the bed.

"They want to keep you for observation, so you have to stay another night or two," he started. "Shit," he said out loud. This wasn't going to be easy.

David moved to the bed and, after informing Michael he was going to sit down, gently lowered his six-foot-two-inch frame onto the bed next to Michael. He gently took Michael in his arms and softly touched his lips to the bruised cheek.

"Sweetheart, I'm afraid there's more bad news," David began. "The asshole who did this to you also burned your house down. At least, that's what the police believe."

David felt Michael inhale sharply and then begin to tremble violently. He pulled Michael closer. "I'm sorry, baby," David said, trying to console his friend.

The hospital room door whooshed open, and David looked up. The man who seemed to blow into the room was short, about five eight. Where David was tall, with olive complexion and thick ebony hair, the man who had burst into the room was the opposite; his ruddy complexion clashed with the carrot-red of his hair. He was stocky where

David was lean and toned. David was handsome while he was strikingly plain.

"Well, I knew it!" the man said in mock horror as he moved around the bed to where David was sitting. "I leave you two alone for a minute, and you have a torrid affair. Hate to tell you this, Michael, but he's married with triplets."

Michael reached out, and the man grasped the proffered hand. David watched as tears rolled down the man's freckled face. With his free hand, the man reached over and took David's.

David smiled at the man who then leaned up on his toes to kiss him gently on the lips. "Good morning, Kelly," he whispered into the kiss.

"Hello," Kelly replied, the sadness on his face not showing in his voice. "Michael, I am here to keep you out of trouble, and I see I wasn't a moment too soon. I love you, but really, this handsome doctor is mine."

There had not been a sound or movement from Michael, and David made no comments.

"I'll come back later and check on you," David told Michael and then turned to Kelly. "Where are the kids?" he asked his husband of ten years.

"I have them at the synagogue. It's Mother's day out today, so I have a sitter until two this afternoon. Then Maria will pick them up and take them home. I'll get home about four. When will you be home?" Kelly informed and asked David.

"About six."

"Okay, go do your doctor things, and I'll take care of our Miss Thing here."

David kissed Kelly again and then gently kissed Michael's exposed cheek before leaving.

As soon as the door closed, Kelly took the place on the bed that David had vacated. "He told you?" Kelly asked, letting the misery in his heart finally show in his voice.

He watched as Michael's bandaged head nodded.

"Well, it's a setback, but I have it all covered. You don't need to worry. You didn't touch your breakfast," Kelly diverted before continuing. "You remember the 'brownstone' in Montrose on Stanford Street?" Kelly didn't wait for an answer. "Well, David's brother, Daniel, lives there now. He rents it, and he gets a great deal, I might add. It's three bedrooms, and he only uses the first two floors. The master suite's upstairs on the third floor, he doesn't use it at all. The cleaning lady told me he hardly ever goes up there."

Kelly spooned some applesauce and instructed Michael to take a bite. Satisfied after Michael had had three spoonfuls of sauce, Kelly continued, "You're going to stay there until you are better and you can get the legal shit with the insurance taken care of and can get you a new place to live. I'll come in the morning to help you bathe and tend to your wound care. I am a registered nurse, you know." Kelly added, knowing full well that Michael knew he was. "Also Mrs. Goldman lives next door. She's retired and has agreed to come in after lunch and check up on you. And she is only a minute away at night if you need her. This is all subject to change. I might come at night, and Mrs.

Goldberg comes in the morning, but one of us will be there for you."

Not stopping to give Michael a chance to argue, Kelly went on, "Daniel is never home. His job keeps him away, and he really can't say anything because he pays nearly nothing for that house. Besides, I keep his refrigerator stocked and his house clean. Without me, he would starve and live in a pigsty."

Before Kelly could say anything else, the day-shift nurse came in to check Michael's stats, signaling Kelly to say good-bye. With as much flourish as she had entered the room, Kelly promised to return later and left.

Daniel glared at his serviceable wristwatch as he opened the door that led from the garage to the kitchen. It was two in the morning. He was exhausted; he hadn't showered or shaved in two days. He glanced at the answering machine on the wall, twelve messages. He was too damned tired to give a shit who had called. What he wanted now was a beer, a shower, then bed. He took off his watch and placed it in the basket on the granite countertop next to the garage door. Then he added his keys and cell phone, noticing it too had messages he hadn't bothered to check before setting the alarm.

The house smelled clean. Mrs. Martinez, the housekeeper, came every Friday. Even at two on a Sunday morning, the house still smelled clean. He enjoyed coming home to a clean house. He didn't pay Mrs. Martinez;

his brother and Kelly did. Also, when Dan opened the refrigerator, he found it stocked with fresh food and a six-pack of beer. "Kelly," Dan said to the contents of the refrigerator, "if you weren't already taken and a guy, I'd marry you."

Taking two beers out of the refrigerator, Dan went through the open floor plan of the first floor and took the stairs to the second floor.

The second floor had two bedrooms and two bathrooms. The third floor had the master suite, with its overlarge bedroom, bathroom, and sitting room. It was nice, but when David and Kelly had moved out, Dan had left the furniture and decorations as they had been. So now, the bedroom was used when their parents came from DC to visit the grandkids. The rest of the house had had a neutral masculinity to it, so Dan kept to the bottom two floors.

He took a moment to lock away his gun and badge before he began to strip, leaving a trail of clothes as he went from the bedroom door to the bathroom. He set his beers on the back of the toilet, and after turning on the water and adjusting the multiple showerheads to massage his aching body, he opened a bottle and, in several long pulls, emptied it.

The heat and pulsating spray of the shower, along with the beer, began to ease Dan's tension. He soaped up and rinsed two days of sweat down the drain. He had been on "loan" to the Galveston County Sheriff's Department. As soon as he walked in to the precinct headquarters that Friday morning, they had shipped him off to Galveston. He was somewhat of an "expert" in communication. Actually, his first language had been ASL, American Sign Language, and to the law enforcement agencies in the Greater Houston Metropolitan area, having a detective who was also a certified interpreter made him somewhat of a valuable commodity.

Dan didn't feel like one; he was too tired to think about something that came naturally for him. Both his parents and both sets of grandparents were deaf; they also were teachers at the university level. They had expected hard work and good professions from their sons. David was a general practitioner who employed a signing staff and whose clientele were, in large part, from the deaf community. Likewise, Dan had finished Harvard Law School but had changed his mind, much to his family's dismay, after passing the bar and had gone into law enforcement instead. He had moved to Houston to be near his brother. Naturally his parents had been upset, but Dan still worked in and with the deaf community. Making sure they were treated with as much respect and understanding as their hearing contemporaries were treated had appeased them.

Fifteen minutes later, Dan stepped out of the shower. He dried off and opened his second beer. He took his time savoring the taste before finishing. Then he brushed his teeth and crawled into bed.

He lay there for a moment, testing the air. Mrs. Martinez must have used a new carpet freshener or a different furniture polish. The air had a fresh floral scent to it. It was nice, Dan thought to himself. He didn't have to be at work until ten Monday morning, so he was going to enjoy a full day of sleep, football, and beer.

The first-class lounge at Houston's George Bush Intercontinental Airport was sparsely populated with travelers at this early hour of a Sunday morning. The ridiculously tall and perfectly coiffed hostess glided across the plush room and cleared her throat. "Excuse me," she purred in her East Texas twang.

Catfish looked up from his coffee and *New York Times* and smiled up at the woman. He had watched her since he had arrived at five fifteen and knew her type. She could sniff out a successful, moneyed man from across a room, and she had.

In an equally strong but different Southern accent, Catfish inquired, "Yes, ma'am?"

"You had asked me to inform you when it was six thirty, sir," she said.

"Thank you. My plane leaves in forty-five minutes. If you could come back in ten minutes, I would really appreciate it."

"Certainly, sir," Ramona Hicks, as her name tag informed all those who cared to look, said as she returned to her post.

Catfish had remained in Houston, taking care of business both personal and professional. He was a man of details and understood that his reasons for being in Houston had to be legitimate. Each night, as he always did, he had called his wife and children. He had kept the meetings his secretary had scheduled for him over the previous months. But now Catfish needed to return home for a few days.

Ten minutes later, Ms. Hicks returned, placing her manicured hands neatly over the back of the luxurious winged-back chair opposite where Catfish sat. He knew her game; she wanted to let him know, by the ringlessness of her fingers, that perhaps, if the enticements were right, she could be had. *What I would do to you, you would never survive!* Catfish thought to himself as he thanked her and began gathering his things.

As he headed for the heavy wood doors that led out into the concourse, she asked, “Mr. Morris, did you enjoy your stay in our lovely city?”

At her words, Catfish turned to face her, “Sweetheart,” he answered giving her one of his special smiles, “I did!”

She watched as the man left the lounge. She had thought him nice and, although not handsome in anyway, at least interesting looking. But as she lowered herself to one of the many chairs throughout the lounge, she realized she was shaking. The smile, the smile that had been on his face just before he had left the lounge was that of a monster. She prayed she would never see him or that smile again.

CHAPTER 2

It was the smell of coffee brewing that initially woke Dan. With one eye, he glimpsed the clock on the nightstand and groaned when the number displayed 6:43 a.m. If this was some twisted scheme of Kelly's, Dan was going to kill him. Yet something hadn't seemed right when he had lain down last night, and something didn't seem right now. The atmosphere of the condo had changed, and Dan couldn't put his finger on it. Not just yet!

If it was Saturday, Dan could have understood someone setting the coffee to begin brewing early, but it was Sunday. He was sure he had set the alarm so if someone had gotten into the house via the main floor doors or windows, he would have known, unless it was his brother or Kelly. Despite all this nagging at him, Dan's sleep-fogged brain couldn't seem to worry about the coffeepot or even the security alarm.

He went back to sleep.

The sounds of something breaking and water running shot Dan out of bed. He reached for and hurriedly unlocked the lockbox with his gun on the floor next to the bed. He also, as an afterthought, quietly pulled a pair of boxers out of the dresser, stopping in the center of the bedroom, hurriedly pulled on the boxers and listened.

The noise had come from the third floor. The water sounded like the shower. Carefully, Dan headed up the stairs. As he topped the stairs, he could see that the bed had been slept in. A pair of sweatpants, his sweatpants, lay on the floor.

He wondered if David and Kelly had had an argument and one of them had come and spent the night. It had never happened before. His brother and Kelly were truly happy. In fact, Dan didn't know a couple, straight or gay, who had as good a relationship as they had.

Slowly, Dan moved toward the bathroom. The door was open, and he could hear the water as it poured out of the bath faucet. Cautiously, Dan looked around the doorjamb and into the bathroom.

He straightened and stared into the large room. A coffee mug had been dropped, shattering and spilling coffee on the marble floor. A woman, naked, stood frozen between the tub/shower and the sink, the broken mug and coffee pooled at her feet.

Dan looked at her, not as a man would look at a naked woman, but as a police detective would look at a victim of a crime. She was about five seven and had a shapely, well-toned body that was covered with bruises. The bruise pattern on her thighs suggested possible sexual assault. He had seen them before. Her chest was black and blue. Over her right breast was a cut that ran across the top curve. Her face, what was not covered with a swatch of gauze, was swollen and discolored. She probably had a broken nose that had been reset at the hospital because there was no definition to her facial features. What was visible of the top of her head had no hair but was beginning to show dark stubble. She turned around in a tight circle, keeping her feet in the same place. This gave Dan the chance to see the old and new wounds on her back. *Shit,* Dan thought to himself, ***what sick bastard did this?***

Dan calmed his nerves. This had Kelly's name written all over it. Kelly was always picking up strays and finding them homes, so why not a stray woman?

"Don't be frightened," Dan said in his most comforting voice. "I'm not gonna hurt you. My name is Dan Hartman. This is my house."

The woman froze, lifting her head toward the sound of his voice. She didn't try to cover herself but stood as if waiting.

"I don't want you to move. The broken mug is all over the floor, and if you move, you might cut your feet. I'm going to go get some shoes on, bring a robe for you to put on, and then clean this mess up. I'll be right back. Don't move."

Dan flew down the stairs. He slipped into some deck shoes and then grabbed a robe from his bathroom door. After making a stop in the laundry room on the first floor to get a broom and dustpan, Dan returned to the bathroom.

The woman hadn't moved.

"I'm coming closer and I have a robe. I want you to hold out your arm so I can give it to you. Then, I am going to pick you up and move you away from all the pieces of that broken mug, so I can clean up. If that's ok, I need you to tell me."

She slowly nodded her head and reached out her hands. Dan handed her the robe which she slowly put on over her battered body.

"Okay, now I'm going to reach for you. Are you ready?" He didn't want there to be any reason for her to be stressed anymore than she probably was.

She nodded again.

Dan explained to her every move he was making, keeping a running stream of dialogue going. She didn't respond. When he had lifted her up into his arms, she relaxed into him, making him aware all he was wearing was his boxers.

Dan took her out of the bathroom and, after explaining that he was going to place her on the bed, did so. "I'll be right back."

Dan returned to the bathroom to clean up the broken mug. He placed the shards into the trash and, using a bath towel, mopped up the spilled coffee. He also turned off the running water in the tub. He noticed the coffeepot had been moved into the bathroom. There was still enough for several cups. A collection of mugs guarded the pot, so Dan poured himself and the woman a cup before returning to the bedroom.

She had dressed in the sweat suit that had been on the floor. It was inside out, but he wasn't going to say a word.

"I brought you another cup of coffee," Dan said.

She reached out her hand and accepted the coffee blindly.

He stood several feet away from her, studying her. What the hell was he supposed to do with her? Kelly! Dan was going to call Kelly and see just what the hell was going on.

"I'm going to take a shower. I would like you not to go back into the bathroom with that cup. I'll be back in about fifteen minutes. If you need something, just yell. I'll be right here," Dan told her, backing out of the room. He was going to kill both of them.

Kelly answered the phone on the second ring. Sunday was their day off, the kids were still asleep, and he wanted to enjoy what little rest he could get. David had gotten home later than usual, so they had gotten to bed almost at midnight. It had always been their way to spend Saturday nights as adult time. So after the kids were down for the night, David and he could do the things that loving couples did when their kids were asleep.

"Hello," Kelly spoke sleepily into the phone.

"Hello, my ass," Dan's voice bellowed. "There is a naked half-beaten woman in my house. Why don't I know anything about this?"

"Dan, sweetheart," Kelly announced in his sweetest tone, which should have been Dan's first clue he had pissed off the wrong person. "First of all, if you look at the photo I put on your dresser, you will see what that woman really looks like. I wanted you to put a face on over the bandages. Secondly, you don't sleep with me or help raise my kids, therefore, you can kiss my freckled and ruddy ass. Here's your brother."

Kelly turned to David, kicking him awake. "It's your brother, and he is pissed because he doesn't know about the woman in his house. Talk to him." Kelly thrust the phone into David's hand and rolled back over.

"Good morning, Dan," David said in his best bedside manner after taking a moment to wake up.

"Fuck you," Dan barked.

"Okay, but before you start with this bullshit, listen to me. I left messages for you starting on Thursday afternoon until Saturday at the precinct, on your cell and on the answering machine at the house. So if you didn't know you have a visitor, that's your problem, not mine. Secondly, she is not a stranger. That is Michael Braun."

Dan sputtered an interruption, "The Michael that works for you? The Michael, which you have known and talked about forever? That Michael? The Michael I just assumed was a man."

"Yes, that Michael, and you know what they say about assumptions," David shot back. "Ass!"

Ignoring his brother's sarcasm, Dan asked, "What the hell happened to her?" his tone changing from anger to concern.

"She was attacked," David simply said. How else could he say it? "It was only logical that since we had a place for her to stay, she should stay there. But don't worry, Mrs. Goldman will be by at nine to help her dress. Her dressings need to be changed. Kelly and I will be by later today to check up on her and give her some pain meds to help her sleep. You don't have to do anything but be nice."

Sure, I can be nice, he thought sarcastically to himself. "Is there anything else I need to know? I mean she is fine, despite the beating she took?" Dan asked his brother.

"There is only one thing that you need to know. Michael is mute but can hear. She uses ASL to communicate, so don't expect to hear her yell at your stupidity or anything."

"Great, I told her if she needed anything, yell and I would be right there," Dan said.

David could hear his embarrassment. A little humbling wouldn't hurt him.

"Wait! Why can't she talk?" he asked again, his tone showing real curiosity.

David sighed, "I don't know why I should fucking tell you this, but maybe it will help you not be such an asshole!"

Dan wanted to protest but knew better.

"When she was born," David began, "she had some respiratory problems. The nurse or doctor in the small hospital didn't know how to or didn't pay attention, but basically they messed up her voice box. She should be able to speak. Lucky she didn't have enough damage to keep her breathing or eating functions from being normal. She thinks, and I agree, that it was too painful to make vocal sounds when she was a baby, and so she didn't." There was a pause before David added, "If you don't use it, you lose it . . . like your brain, brother! Good-bye, Dan," David said and hit the off button on the phone.

"Everything okay?" Kelly asked as he scooted into David.

"It'll be better soon," David whispered into Kelly's ear then kissed his neck.

Dan hung up the phone and ran his fingers through his hair. This was not how he wanted to start his day off, but he didn't seem to have a choice in the matter. He decided the best thing to do was to dress and then maybe fix them something to eat. After Mrs. Goldman came to help Michael, he could either go back to bed or . . . hell, he wasn't sure.

Dan took a few minutes to dress in old jeans and a T-shirt, brush his teeth, and wash his face. Then remembering what Kelly had said, he turned to his dresser and found a large 8 × 10 of Michael.

The photo was of a strikingly beautiful and exotic woman. She must have been at a formal dinner since she was wearing the infamous "little black dress." It showed off the fullness of her breasts, the flat stomach, the curves of her hips, her surprisingly long, shapely legs and all but screamed the word "sex" back at him. Her hair was thick, wavy ebony tresses that clashed with the porcelain complexion of her face. Her eyes were wide and framed with thick dark lashes, and she looked down and away from the camera. Her nose was narrow and straight, her cheekbones high, her lips obscenely full. There was a slightly crooked smile on her lips that lit up her face.

It was a face that Dan remembered. He had seen that face, that body, before at a party of David's once. He was leaving as she was coming in, and they bumped into each other. She had given him a "melt your pants off" smile and had kissed him not so chastely on the lips then had mouthed, "You look hot!" He had been dumbfounded as to why this sexy woman had kissed him. Dan remembered thinking at that time if he hadn't had a date with him, he would have gone back inside. It had never dawned on him that exotic beauty had been Michael.

Now he cursed Kelly. Kelly knew him too well. He knew what response the picture would have. It had put pieces of conversations together in Dan's mind. He had heard about Michael for eleven, maybe twelve years. Michael and David had done this, or Michael and David had done that. How the triplets loved Michael, what a really special person Michael was in David and Kelly's life. David had touted Michael's work with the battered children and other charities that worked with children.

Now he was hooked. Dan felt that he, on some level, had known Michael as long as David. Maybe, vicariously, he did.

As he walked up the stairs to the third floor, he called out, "Michael, it's Dan. I'm coming up." When he topped the stairs, Michael had redressed her battered body, turning the garments right side out. She also seemed to have brushed her teeth as well because there was a small amount of toothpaste still on the corner of her mouth.

"Michael, David told me that Mrs. Goldman will be here around nine to look after you. It's a little after seven, so until then, how about some more coffee and breakfast?" Dan asked as he went into the bathroom and retrieved a face towel. "You have something here on the corner of your mouth," he said as he gently dabbed at her mouth. She didn't flinch. Dan thought that a bit strange considering what she had been through in what must have been only a few days before.

Dan watched as Michael took a breath, squared her shoulders, and signed, “It is nice to meet you, Dan. I feel as if I’ve known you since David talks about his ‘baby brother’ all the time. Sorry the conditions are so shitty.”

Dan laughed. He supposed that being ten minutes younger made him the baby, but at thirty-five, he didn’t feel much like a baby.

“I would love some breakfast,” Michael added.

Because her face was swollen and bandaged, there was no expression along with her signs. It was as monotone and flat as any bored college professor; therefore, Dan could not be sure if she was indeed happy about a seven o’clock breakfast or not.

CHAPTER 3

After six days with her eyes covered with both patches and bandages, Michael had gotten used to moving around in the darkness. Even though she had been in the condo many times over the years, both Kelly and Mrs. Goldman had helped her get reacquainted with the third floor's layout as well as the rest of the house. So she had been able to move about from room to room and floor to floor. A stereo was situated in the study area of the master suite design, and Kelly had hot-glued beads at the controls so Michael could find the volume and the on/off switch.

Between Kelly, David, and Mrs. Goldman, Michael had had three meals prepared and fresh fruit to snack on. Her mouth was still tender, her face still stiff and sore, but each day, she was feeling better.

Because she had known David for so many years, she felt comfortable with Dan. It was odd, she thought, as he led her down to the kitchen, that although David talked about his brother all the time, she really didn't know anything about him. She knew where he lived, that he was a lawyer, and that he was not gay, but other than that, she knew nothing.

"What do you want for breakfast? Kelly keeps me rather well-stocked, so it can be as easy as cereal or as extravagant as eggs Benedict. I don't know if David told you, but I am a hell of a cook," Dan informed her with a light tone in his voice.

His voice was so similar to his brother's. Even though there was a harder edge to it, it soothed her.

When they had reached the bottom of the stairs, Michael told Dan to surprise her. He led her to a stool that from memory Michael knew was situated at the opposite end of the island from the range. "I'll go get the coffeepot and make some fresh coffee. After that I'll make something to please our sleepy palates."

Michael listened as he left the room and headed upstairs. She followed his footsteps as he returned.

He was being nice to her, which, considering she had heard his conversation with Kelly and David, sort of surprised her.

"I know that my being here wasn't your idea. If you want me to get out of your hair, I will." Michael leveled with Dan, signing in the direction she hoped Dan was when she heard his return.

When he didn't answer, she slapped her hand on the marble top of the bar, paused a few seconds, and started to repeat her last comment, "I know—"

"I heard you the first time, Michael." There was a pause. "You are right, your being here isn't my idea, but I agree with my brother that this is a good place for you to be."

She didn't really know what to say. "I'll stay out of your way. The bandages come off in two days, and I will be able to keep the house clean or cook meals or whatever to earn my keep."

Dan interrupted her, "You don't have to do anything but get your life back together. Believe it or not, I understand how traumatizing this can be for someone. I see it all the time. Besides, if I turned you into my personal housekeeper and cook, the Smyth-Hartmans and Mrs. Martinez would kill me. And you are aware how Kelly can be if he gets on a roll."

Michael laughed. It was a breathy noise void of vocal sounds, and to some people, it was uncomfortable to see her laugh.

"You have a nice laugh," she heard Dan say.

Michael stopped laughing, snapping her jaw shut. No one had ever said that to her before, and she was somehow uncomfortable. She jokingly signed, "I know. It goes well with my head-on-crash-with-a-semi look."

Dan grew silent as he made breakfast. The sound of pots and pans being used and the smell of different foods as they were being prepared only deepened the silence. For several long minutes, neither spoke.

"Look, I wasn't joking. I know it's weird, but I can tell that when you aren't all, well, as you said, sporting that 'head-on-crash-with-a-semi look,' your laughter is real, and it's nice," Dan said. Michael could tell that his back was to her as the sound of his voice seemed to bounce back to her.

The sound of a plate being placed before her brought Michael back from her thoughts. Normally, she would have been embarrassed by what Dan had said but wasn't.

"It's eggs, hash browns, and toast. The eggs at six, the hash browns at nine, and the toast at two. I hope you like scrambled eggs."

"They're my all-time favorite food in the world," Michael lied.

"Mine too," Dan said.

They ate in companionable silence.

Dan had gotten up to refill their coffee cups while explaining to Michael what he was doing. Michael supposed he was doing it so she wouldn't be surprised by his movements. She appreciated that.

"So," Michael signed, as she pushed her plate away, "what kind of law do you practice?" She remembered David telling her that Dan had a law degree.

"My degree was in criminal law, but I'm not a lawyer. After I passed the bar, I decided being a lawyer wasn't what I wanted to do, so I became a police officer. I'm a detective now."

Michael stilled. She had a deep distrust and unease with regard to the police, and the knowledge that Dan was a cop made Michael apprehensive. She didn't know what to do or how to react to this information. On one hand, she could be mad at David and Kelly for not being totally truthful with her; on the other hand, she never asked for clarification, thinking it would never be important.

The best thing, she decided, was to keep to herself and act as if she didn't care. Michael was an expert at being alone in a crowded room.

Dan must have noticed the change in her demeanor. "I promise I'm the good kind of cop," he said.

"You know how it is" was the only thing Michael could think to say.

"Yeah, I do," Dan agreed reluctantly.

She reached for her plate and, because she had been in the house many times and knew the layout of the kitchen, headed for the sink. Michael felt Dan's hand on her elbow as he stopped her and took the plate from her.

"Don't worry about it. I'll take care of it. You just relax." There was a pause. Then Dan asked, "Look, I know it's none of my business, but where did this happen? The reason I'm asking is maybe there is something I can do to help. I could call in a few favors, get an update and information about what's going on with your investigation."

This was exactly what Michael didn't want. It was bad enough that David and possibly Kelly had seen her charts and knew everything that had been done to her in the past, but she didn't want this man, whom she really didn't know, getting involved any more than he already was.

"Thank you, but I have to go to the precinct office Tuesday to talk to the investigating officer. He came to see me in the hospital, but David only let him stay a few minutes. There's not anything to tell, I don't remember anything." Michael stood up and, turning her head in the direction of Dan's voice, told him she was going to go lie down.

Michael's day went as it had since she had come to the house on Stanford five days before. At nine, Mrs. Goldman came and helped her bathe, something she had been trying to do for herself earlier that morning. Then her eyes were flushed out and new bandages applied. Additionally, the sutures on her head, her face, and her breast were checked for infection. Afterward, Michael listened as Mrs. Goldman chatted about whatever was on the older woman's mind.

Today it had been her sister-in-law. Mrs. Goldman's brother had passed away several years ago, and his wife had taken up with a man in his fifties while she was almost seventy. It had scandalized the family. It took everything in her power to keep Michael from silently giggling. She understood that different generations looked at life events differently; however, she was concerned that Ruthie, as Kelly had called her, was going to have a stroke.

After a light lunch, eaten upstairs in the sitting room of the third floor, Ruthie gave Michael her afternoon dose of antibiotics, wished her good afternoon, and left Michael with instructions to have David or Kelly contact her if there were any changes in the routine for the next few days.

Michael knew Tuesday she had an appointment with both the ophthalmologist and the investigating officer on her case but didn't interrupt her as Ruthie called out her good-bye.

At around seven, Michael heard Kelly's voice as he headed up the stairs. As she listened to Kelly ascend the stairs, she could hear the shrill giggles of the triplets as someone, most likely their uncle, chased them around.

Since the kids were the biological children of David and Kelly's sister, they had Kelly's freckles and red hair, David's dark brown eyes and were deaf.

Michael stood up and walked from the lounge chair to the foot of the bed to wait for Kelly.

"Hello, beautiful," he said as he pecked her cheek. "How was your day?"

Michael wanted to bitch that she had learned that Dan was a cop and was not really too happy about it and that her head and her back itched as if she had fleas. Also, she was going a bit stir crazy with the bandages over her eyes. Instead, she informed Kelly, "I can't wait to take a real bath."

"Well, soon you should be able to do that. Just continue to do as you have been, filling the tub only deep enough to cover your feet and sponge yourself from there. I'll get you some bubble bath that won't hurt your cuts, scrapes, bruises, and other boo-boos. How does that sound?" Kelly's voice moved around her as he spoke.

"Off with the shirt!" Kelly said and his hands pulled at her sleeve.

While Michael took off her shirt, Kelly chattered, "So you met, Dan." He said flatly.

Michael nodded.

"Well, they are both so much alike and so different, I get confused. I don't know if I want to convert him or kill him." Kelly laughed at his own joke while his hands skimmed over Michael's back. "He gets so macho bullshitty sometimes. Maybe it's because he's a cop, or I guess it comes from having a brother who is gay, but please, my brothers don't act that way."

Kelly and Ruthie had a lot in common. Michael knew the best course of action was to just listen.

"Your back is looking better. You won't be wearing a bikini anytime soon, but the cuts are healing up nicely. Ruthie's doing a good job. Okay, let me come around so I can check out your tits."

This time Michael did laugh. She dutifully stood in place as Kelly did his inspection. She felt his hand as it touched her bruised breasts. Along with the cut across the top of one breast, her attacker had done some deep tissue bruising, nothing that wouldn't heal. Kelly had explained that David wanted to make sure that the blood in the contusion was dissipating.

"Kelly, David said to . . . " Dan's voice trailed off then, "What the hell are you doing?"

Michael stood in place with her hands on Kelly's shoulders as he turned slowly around then backed up against her. Unlike this morning when he had found her naked in the bathroom, Michael was uncomfortable with having him in the room with her so exposed. The heat of Kelly's back against her bare breasts did nothing to reduce the uncovered feeling.

"I would tell you, but it is nurse/patient privilege. I don't have to tell you why *I* was fondling Michael's exquisite breasts. You're just jealous that it's my hands and not yours."

Michael would have knocked Kelly to his knees if she'd had on a shirt. As it was, all she could do to him was pinch his shoulder really hard!

"If you're going to abuse me, I'm leaving. Dan, get back downstairs. Tell the doctor, I'm almost done here," Kelly's voice said into the direction of Michael's face. "You're doing fine. Here's your shirt. Now, I want you in bed before eleven, do you understand? David would come up, but we don't want the kids to see their auntie Michael like this."

Michael had a snide comment ready to go until Kelly's last comment. "I love you, guys."

"We know." Michael felt a brief squeeze of her hand then another kiss on the cheek, followed by descending footsteps.

From the third floor, Michael could hear as the triplets were rounded up and David and Kelly made their way out of the condo. A short time later, Dan yelled up the stairs that he had made some spaghetti and a salad for dinner if she was interested.

She was.

The meal was a pleasant surprise. Along with the salad and spaghetti was a loaf of hot Italian bread and some wine, the latter, she couldn't have. Dan, however, poured her some sparkling grape juice, which, also to her surprise, she enjoyed.

"Are you going to work tomorrow?" Michael asked as she ate, signing with one hand. This, being able to have a conversation with your mouth full, was one of the advantages of not using your mouth to have the conversation. "The only reason I am asking is I just want to know your schedule so I can keep out of your hair."

She heard Dan clear his throat. "Look," he stated with a hint of irritation in his voice, "I don't mind that you're here. In fact, it's been nice having someone in the house. I've been thinking about getting a roommate, and this will help me decide if someone can stand to live with me." His laughter lightened the tone. "My normal schedule is Tuesday through Saturday. That changes from time to time. For example, tomorrow I have to go in and finish up some paperwork. So I'll go in early in the morning and be back about two."

For the rest of the meal, they discussed David, Kelly, and the kids. It was light and easy, and Michael was relaxed. Afterward, Dan cleaned the kitchen and got Michael to talk about her job.

"I'm an RN. I met David in medical school. We didn't have the same classes, but he was my boyfriend's roommate. It was nice to meet someone who could sign who wasn't an interpreter and I could have a conversation with, so we became really close. Anyway, when he finished his internship and had decided to go into practice, he hired me to work for him. I actually introduced Kelly to him. We were all at Baylor together, but David didn't know Kelly, and Kelly didn't know David. I knew them both. Kelly and I finished nursing school together. David and I were sharing an apartment in Waco when he came out. I knew already he was never really in the closet to me. Kelly on the other hand was always out and I thought it would be nice if I could introduce my two best friends to each other. The rest, as they say, is history."

"I've heard that story before. I could never figure out why David didn't hook up with you." Michael heard Dan laugh nervously, "I just figured that with a name like Michael you were a guy. You know it's funny," Dan commented as he led Michael to the sofa. "I never met you in all this time. David is always talking about you, and I knew you two were close, but I could have passed you on the street and never known who you were. Even when he used 'her' and 'she,' well, I just thought it was a gay thing."

"You never came to the house or any of the parties, and you weren't at their wedding." Michael was also surprised they had never met.

"That's not true. I went to a few, but their parties aren't the kind of parties I normally go to. I even saw you once as I was leaving. Of course, I didn't know it was you. I was in California when they got married and couldn't make it home to Baltimore for the wedding. David was cool with that. We had a long discussion about it. I know he wanted me to be his best man, and I wanted to, but I had an unexpected murder lead show up."

"I know. David told me you couldn't get home because of your job. Still, it is funny that after a decade we finally meet, and it's really under the worst possible circumstances," Michael added, shrugging her shoulders.

"It'll get better, but now I have to put you to bed," Dan said as Michael felt the glass being removed from her hand.

"It's early," Michael said.

Dan laughed. "No, it's ten thirty."

The night had flown by. Michael was shocked.

"I have a pill David gave to me to give to you. You stay here, and I'll be back."

Michael felt the cushions of the sofa shift as David got up. After a few moments, he returned, handed her a glass, and placed a small pill into her other hand. "Now, take that, and then I'll get you to the stairs. If you need anything, just stomp on the floor . . . no, wait."

He got up again, and Michael could hear him opening and closing drawers in the kitchen. "Found it," Dan said as he sat back down. Michael took the pill and offered the glass to the air and felt it being removed.

"This was a joke, but now it's perfect. Hold out your hand," Dan instructed.

Doing as she was asked, Michael held out her hand and felt the cool metal against her palm. With both hands, she felt its shape and had to laugh. Taking the slender end in her hand, Michael rang the small bell.

"If it works . . . " Dan's voiced started then trailed off into laughter. "Look, I have a few things to do before I head off to bed. David told me that pill works pretty fast, so why don't you head upstairs. Okay?"

"Good idea," Michael agreed and headed to bed. By the time she had changed into her pajamas that Kelly picked up for her at the store, brushed her teeth, and used the facilities one last time, the effect of the pill was making itself known. She felt her way to the bed and crawled under the covers.

Sometime later, Michael wasn't sure if it was ten minutes or two hours; she thought she remembered Dan standing over her, asking if she was all right or if she needed anything. Michael didn't remember her reply but dreamed he had kissed her gently on the lips good-night.

CHAPTER 4

Monday, Michael woke to the smell of coffee and Dan informing her he would see her later. Soon after that, Ruthie showed up for her morning rituals. After lunch, Kelly relieved Ruthie and tended to her until around five. Before leaving, Kelly had prepared dinner, explaining to Michael how to instruct Dan on the finishing touches.

Dan's day was as normal as Michael's. He arrived at the station house to finish with the stack of paperwork on his desk but was pulled into an interrogation. The man who had been picked up for possession of a controlled substance with intent to sell had been assigned an interpreter, but the captain wanted to make sure that everything that was signed was interpreted correctly. So for two hours, Dan stood behind a one-way mirror.

The interpreter, a young woman in her early twenties, had done an excellent job. Dan could find no fault with either her interpretation of the questions or the answers, and Dan informed his boss of that fact.

After spending the entire morning doing something he had no intention of doing, Dan was able to sit at his desk and clear up about a week's worth of paperwork. Several times he had wanted to text Michael and ask how she was doing but stopped himself each time. He had known the woman for one twenty-four-hour period, and already she seemed to have taken over his thoughts. He did, however, send her a brief text at about two thirty to let her know he would be home later than anticipated.

Dan knew that it was unfair to blame Michael, but nonetheless, it was the only way he could keep his mind on his work and off her. He wasn't even sure what it was about her that he kept thinking. What he could see of her face, which was black and blue and swollen. All her hair was cut off, leaving dark stubble covering the part of her head that was exposed from the bandage wrapped around it.

Her body, while something out of a magazine, was also cut, bruised, and bandaged. So what was it? Perhaps it was the photo on his dresser and the memory of Michael as she glided past him all those years ago or the taste of her lips as they had brushed his. Maybe it was her ease around him or the fact that when he had picked her up from the shards of the ceramic mug that covered the bathroom floor, she had melted into his arms. That trust had unsettled him as did the intelligent, sharp, and often funny way she held up a conversation.

But maybe, he tried to convince himself, just maybe, it was a normal reaction to being a police officer and seeing a woman who had been violated and brutalized. "Or a man attracted to a beautiful sexy woman," a voice whispered in his head. The fact that Michael and his brother were such good friends meant that Dan couldn't help but have some concern for her progress. That train of thought pacified him for the rest of the afternoon.

He called his brother around 4:00 p.m. to inquire about where the attack had happened. David told him the attack had happened outside his clinic in the parking garage. With that information, Dan called the precinct and asked to speak with the officer in charge of her case.

"Officer Boudreaux," a gruff voice, thick with a Cajun accent, snarled into the phone.

"Hey, Boudreaux, this is Hartman at the Houston PD, Katy office."

"What can I do for you, Hartman?" The officer's voice lost a little of his brashness.

Dan was hoping that knowing that he was a fellow officer should relax Boudreaux enough for Dan to get some information out of him.

"I understand you're working on the Michael Braun assault case. Can I ask you a few questions?" Dan asked, then quickly added, "Ms. Braun is a longtime friend of the family. I understand that while you might not be able to tell me everything I would like to know, you might at least tell me if you have any leads."

Dan heard papers shuffling in the background. Boudreaux cleared his throat, then said, "Off the record?"

"Off the record," Dan agreed.

"This is really a strange one. The attacker beat the living shit out of her but didn't rape her. He could have because she was unconscious when she was discovered, which was strange too. Whoever it was that attacked her and put her body on the trunk of her car, he wanted her to be found. Also it was real personal. You know and I know that in an attack like this, the attacker is really pissed off at the victim. Problem is the victim says she has no idea who the attacker was. Shit, I believe her too."

Dan interrupted, "Any forensic evidence?"

"Nothing to go to a grand jury with. It took place in a parking garage. Nobody saw nothing. There was no trace evidence that can't be placed at the crime scene or the people that she might have come in contact with throughout her day. The people we questioned have all checked out." The deep sigh carried through the phone to Dan's ears.

He had made the very same sound thousands of times when he had had a case where nothing was panning out. Dan was about to thank Boudreaux and guarantee this was just for his own info and would go no further.

"Then there's the thing with her house," Boudreaux continued.

Dan didn't say a thing. He had no idea what the officer was talking about, so he kept his mouth shut. Obviously, Boudreaux wanted to let off some steam, and Dan was going to let him.

"There was so much accelerant throughout the house that by the time the fire trucks arrived, and mind you, the station is only two miles, the house was completely engulfed. The only thing they found there was a disposable cell phone that probably was used as a triggering device. The house went up about the same time that Ms. Braun was getting the living shit kicked out of her. Oh, sorry, I forgot," Boudreaux said, obviously remembering that Dan was a friend.

"That's okay," Dan said and thanked the officer for his help. Dan hung up the phone and stared at it for a few moments. The one thing that stuck in Dan's mind was the comment about the attack being personal. He understood exactly what Boudreaux was saying. Most of the time an attack as violent as the one that Michael had experienced was directed toward her as an individual.

He picked up the receiver again and called his brother. "Doctor's office," a sweet-voiced receptionist purred into the phone.

"Hello, this is Dan Hartman, Dr. Hartman's brother. Could I speak with him for a moment?" Dan poured all his charm into his voice knowing the receptionist knew who he was and it would get him to his brother faster.

"Mr. Hartman, one moment please."

"Dan, what's up?" David's voice said unhurriedly.

"Why didn't you tell me that not only was Michael beaten but also had her house burned down?" He was pleased the anger he felt hadn't made its way into his voice.

"Oh, I really forgot about it. I mean, our main concern has been making sure she was really okay. I don't know what to tell you." There was a pause, and then David added, "Why? Is it a problem that she's in the house? Shit, Dan, the house is huge. I don't see why—"

Dan interrupted, “There isn’t any problem, asshole. I just . . . well, if she . . . damn it, David, I just feel like I should know all there is to know. I mean, here is this woman living in my house, and although you have known her forever, I haven’t.”

“Dan, she isn’t a liar, a thief, or a serial killer. What the fuck is your problem?”

“I don’t know,” Dan said and hung up the phone. He was not sure if that was true.

CHAPTER 5

Dan sat inside his car a long time after the garage door had closed. He looked at the door into the house and wondered why the hell he didn't get out of the car. When he finally did and opened the door into the kitchen, his nostrils were assailed with the mouthwatering aroma of food. The smell was familiar. It was a thick stew that his mother made and had passed the recipe on to Kelly when David and he had gotten together.

The stereo was on the jazz station, and the table was set for two. Dan didn't know if he wanted to stay or leave. Michael's appearance coming down the stairs helped him decide.

She was dressed in black slacks and an overlarge shirt that he recognized again as one of his own. She seemed to be wearing a lot of his clothes, and damn, did she look good in them.

Her head was unbandaged although there were tan patches over her eyes. It had been eight days since the attack, and the color of the bruises were at their height. Only on her exposed arms was the black and blue fading into lighter shades with yellow mixed into the palette.

As Dan moved into the kitchen and Michael moved toward him, he noticed that she was barefooted, and her toenails were painted a shocking red.

"Dan, is that you?" Michael asked. The fluidness of her movements reminded him of how both his mother and father signed, gracefully and artistically.

"Yeah. Who did all the cooking?" What Dan really wanted to know was if Michael was aware of the layout that had been set up.

"Kelly told me he was cooking a stew and there was a salad in the refrigerator. He also told me to tell you he knows what he is doing and don't change a thing. I'm just the messenger and haven't a clue what he was talking about, so don't blame me."

Dan watched as Michael moved to the bar and took a seat. "If you tell me what needs to be done, I can help."

"No, I'll do it. Tomorrow after the doctor takes those bandages off your eyes, you can help if you want. But for now, just enjoy the break. How was your day?"

"Oh, you know. Shopping, a day at the spa, that sort of thing." Even without the voice, her body language allowed the sarcasm to drip from the comment. "I'm not one to just sit around and do nothing. I like to read but"—Michael motioned to her bandaged covered eyes—"these make it a little difficult to do that. Also, Ruthie, who just left not long ago, makes me take naps. Can you believe that? I know David is behind the whole nap idea, but still she really gets after me if I even look as if I'm going to give her a hard time about it."

Dan laughed as he pulled the stew out of the oven. He had seen ol' Ruthie in action; she could be rather forceful. "I can imagine."

"No, you can't." Michael's movements were insistent.

Dan watched as Michael moved off the barstool to where he was standing in the wide-open space of the kitchen. She bumped into him, and he put his arm around her to steady them both.

"Sorry," Michael said, taking several steps back away from him. "But I'm telling you, my own mother or grandmother never was this tough on me."

Aah! Here was a piece of information. "I want you to go back to your stool, and I'm going to serve up this wonderful meal Kelly made." After resetting the bar with some of the place settings from the table, Dan ladled the stew into two large bowls; he placed the tossed salad, hot bread, and glasses of iced tea on the bar. He relayed to Michael the location of each of the dishes.

"So where are your parents?"

Michael's spoon stopped in midair before she lowered it back to the stew. It was apparent this was not something Michael normally discussed. Her whole body stiffened. Dan was pissed at himself for even asking the question, but he needed to understand where she came from to understand what had happened to her. In police work, you never knew where information would lead you.

"Look, I'm sorry."

"No, it's all right. My parents divorced when I was five and my brother was eight. After that we lived with our mother and grandparents, Mum's," Michael said. She signed "Mother" and clarified by fingerspelling M-U-M, "parents, in Dublin, Ireland," resuming her meal after the information.

"Are you Irish then? I thought everyone Irish was redheaded and freckle-faced?" The voice Dan's imagination had created for Michael immediately changed from a sexy, whiskey-smooth Texas twang to a low sexy Irish accented purr.

"Some are, some aren't." There was a pause then Michael continued, "We were born in the US but carry dual citizenship. When I was eighteen, I returned to the US to go to school, Baylor, and never left. I followed in my brother's footsteps. He returned to go to school and stayed as well. We go back when we can, but our grandparents are busy people, and our mother won't come here to the States. But my grandparents come and visit every other year or so."

"What do they do?"

Michael took a deep breath before answering. "They're both doctors. Grandda is a cardiologist, and Grandma is an endocrinologist."

"What about your brother? What does he do?" Dan asked.

"This stew is really delicious," Michael signed over the bowl of stew.

Dan knew when to drop the subject. "Yes, it is one of my favorites. My mother made it all the time."

The rest of the meal was eaten in strained silence. Dan watched Michael. He knew tomorrow this sort of intense observation would become impossible. With the bandages off her eye, Michael would be aware of this sort of intrusion. He wondered what color her eyes were. The photo on his dresser was good, but for some reason, she had been glancing down effectively masking the color of her eyes.

"How are you feeling?" Dan asked, trailing his hand down her arm. "Are you cold?" He had wanted to touch her. Her skin was as soft as he'd imagine. Jesus, what was the matter with him?

"No," Michael replied as she placed her hand over Dan's. "I'm just tired."

Before Dan could respond, the phone rang.

"Hello," Dan spoke into his cell.

"Hey, bro," David's voice came through the line. "Look, Kelly isn't going to be able to get back and Mrs. Goldman had a thing tonight at her temple, so you're going to have to help out and make sure our girl gets redressed and into bed at a decent time. She has a big day tomorrow, and she's going to need her rest. I want you to make sure she gets that sleeping pill about nine tonight."

"You've got to be shitting me" was the only response Dan could think of.

"No, it's easy. First lower the lights and wash out her eyes with the solution in the bathroom. Then after she has dried her face, replace the eye patches. They're there next to the eye solution. Then I need you to check the sutures on her head and breast and lip. Also the places on her back to make sure there is no infection. There wasn't this afternoon but apply some of the ointment to the wounds. That's it."

Dan wanted to reach through the phone line and strangle his brother. He had had basic first aid and had seen his share of gruesome things in the line of duty, but this was more than he wanted to deal with. The last thing he needed was to see Michael's breast. At the thought of her breast, Dan became hard, making him feel like a pervert.

"I think you need to tell Michael this. If she's okay with it, I'll do it," Dan told David, hoping Michael would have a fit.

She didn't. He wasn't sure what David had said to her. She listened to him, tapping once or twice on the mouthpiece with her spoon. Dan watched as her swollen lips trembled as if she might break down and cry any moment but stopped as she handed the phone in the general direction of Dan.

"Okay, she said that if this was how it had to be, she would get over it," David said almost too gleefully.

"How the fu—— hell did you get that out of tapping on the phone with a spoon?" Dan demanded.

"Easy. Years of practice."

"Right! Okay, do I need to call you back when we're finished?"

"No, not unless you see a problem."

There's a problem already, Dan thought to himself, looking down at his arousal.

After a few more instructions, David hung up. Michael seemed to have lost her appetite as did Dan. He wasn't sure why she had stopped eating, but he knew why he had. Even though Michael was black and blue, swollen and puffy, Dan knew what she really looked like in a little black dress, and that's how he saw her. He wanted her. She had affected him in a very strange way. He had had girlfriends and a fiancé or two over the years, but he had never met a woman whom he wanted to get into bed with and at the same time take care of and just be with until two days ago. His reaction just wasn't natural.

A touch on his face caused him to turn his head toward Michael. "Dan, if this is uncomfortable for you, I can take care of it myself. I won't say anything. Really this isn't your problem."

Shit! She had completely misunderstood his reluctance to do this. "No, Michael, it's fine. It was just a surprise, and I don't want to do anything wrong. You know David, oh god, Kelly. I would never hear the end of it if I as much as allowed an eyelash to go astray."

Michael laughed her soundless laugh, and Dan wanted to kiss her.

Later, when Michael was lying in bed, she thought about the evening and how Dan had done his best to tend to her. Michael had removed her shirt and, using a towel, covered all but the topmost curves of her breasts.

Dan's hand shook as he washed out her eyes in the darkened bathroom. He was quick but thorough, checking the sutures on her head, face, and breast. She lay on her stomach as he checked over her back. With slow, almost painfully slow motions, he rubbed her back with the ointment. His bare leg touched her side, setting fire to her middle. She wanted him to finish before she burst into flames.

She couldn't imagine why the touch of his fingers applying the ointment to the raised marks on her back was causing a stirring deep inside her.

When he was finished, Michael stayed on the bed.

"I hope I didn't hurt you," Dan said, his voice coming from near her face.

She shook her head. She was in pain, but it had nothing to do with the wounds from the attack. She just wanted him to leave. "Thank you," Michael told him, hoping he would take the hint that since she wasn't moving to get up, he could leave.

"OK, then. Good night." His voice was so close; his breath caressed the exposed skin of her cheek. Michael imagined Dan kneeling on the floor, his face level with hers. So near she could have kissed him.

When he finally left, Michael got up and put on a different pair of pj's that Kelly had brought. They were shorts and a tank top, which he told her were decorated with Pooh and Tigger. They were light and allowed for her skin to breathe.

As she drifted off to sleep, Michael's last thought was that tomorrow, she would finally get to see Dan's face.

CHAPTER 6

"Good morning, sleepyhead, time to get your ass outa bed." Kelly's voice boomed from what Michael could only assume was the top of the stairs. "It's already seven thirty, and we have a 9:00 a.m. appointment with Dr. Huang. Then we have to go to the police station and talk with that detective."

Michael flung her feet to the floor and prayed that Kelly had brought up a mug of coffee. He had, and Michael had sent prayers up for the coffee gods. As she sipped her coffee, she heard the water running in the tub and Kelly talking to himself.

She finally got up and carefully moved to the bathroom.

"Strip and get into the tub. I don't want you to get the top of your head wet, but the rest of you can take the water. Test the water to see if it's too hot before you get in. Myself,

I like to boil in the bath." Kelly's hand touched Michael's forearm as he directed her toward the tub.

She stuck her hand under the running water and, after a few minor adjustments, checked it again. Neither ashamed nor embarrassed, Michael stepped out of her pj's and, with Kelly's assistance, lowered herself into the water.

Kelly gently washed her back while Michael bathed the rest.

"I bought you a turtleneck sweater 'cause it's only gonna get to the upper fifties today and it's kind of cool now. Also, I did as you asked me and bought you a pair of jeans. I bought Levi's. I hope that's fine," Kelly informed her as he rinsed off her back.

"Great, as long as it fits, I don't care. I tried on the bra that Rosie got for me, but it is still too painful to wear, so I suppose I could put on a T-shirt under the turtleneck."

"Whatever you want, we just need to hurry." Kelly warned as his voice trailed out of the bathroom, closing the door behind him.

Michael took that as a sign for her to get out of the bath. After finishing her morning toiletries, Michael stepped out of the bathroom. Kelly informed her that her clothes had been laid out on the bed, and he was glad she was getting her eyes back because he was tired of being her manservant. Michael, for her part, ignored him and dressed. She didn't worry about what was laid out for her because she knew Kelly's tastes were impeccable, and he wouldn't dress her in anything less than fashionable.

When she was dressed, she was handed a pair of loafers for her feet. "Where did you get all these clothes?" she asked when she discovered lacy panties and a camisole with her jeans and sweater.

Kelly explained that in her trunk was an overnight bag. Michael had forgotten about her car and the overnight bag. Kelly had rummaged through the bag and, after verifying the sizes, went to the mall and did a bit of shopping.

"It'll do until you feel like going to the mall and shopping for yourself. Also, I bought a webcam for the computer in the second-floor bedroom. You can download your video relay program to that computer so when you are ready, you can use it to start making those phone calls."

As soon as the VP was set up, she would call her brother. Until now she had just been relying on Ruthie to text her brother that she was okay and making good progress.

"I already called your insurance guy, Thom." Kelly continued, "Remember he's our insurance guy too, and I told him about the house. He is already working on the paperwork and told me to tell you to give him a call when you are ready."

Sinking to the bed and feeling tears well up behind the bandages, Michael realized she seemed to have forgotten a lot of things. "My house," she signed, the pain in her heart mirrored in her sign.

"I know, sweetie, but you have a place here for as long as you like." Michael heard Kelly take a deep breath. "Look, today is going to be a hell of a day. So let's get it started so we can finish and get back home."

Michael agreed.

Dr. Huang's office was like any other doctor's office, cold and antiseptic. Michael had asked Kelly to come into the room and act as interpreter. Normally, she would never have asked, but it was easier to have someone who cared about her do this for her. Kelly didn't mind.

The nurse came in to check her vitals and asked her a list of questions. After several minutes, she left the room with the information stating Dr. Huang would be in to see her in a few minutes.

Ten minutes later, the doctor arrived.

"So how are you feeling?" he asked.

Michael repeated all her answers that the nurse had asked and had already documented. She didn't mind; as a nurse herself, she knew the drill.

"I'm going to lower the lights and then remove the bandages from your eyes. Then I'm going to take a look. After I verify there is no damage we can see, I'll have you look at a few objects, all in reduced light. Then if everything is okay, I'll dilate your eyes to check for retinal damage. Now it won't hurt, but you won't be able to focus for about forty-five minutes to an hour. I have some really ugly sunglasses for you to wear. I want you to wear them until you get home. Then I want you to spend the rest of the day indoors with all the blinds closed. Tomorrow, it will be fine for you to go out and start doing everything you normally would do, provided you wear a good pair of sunglasses out in the sunlight."

Dr. Huang stepped away, and Michael heard the click of the light switch continuing his list of requirements as he moved about. "I want you to keep the television watching to a minimum for the next week. Also you can use the computer for about ten minutes a day, and limit your reading to a few minutes each day for the next week or so. After that, everything should be back to normal. If you have any pain or anything that doesn't feel right, call me immediately."

Michael agreed to all Dr. Huang's instructions.

"Are you ready?" the doctor asked.

Michael nodded her head and took a calming breath.

She felt the bandages being removed from her eyes and was warned to keep her eyes closed until she was told to open them.

"Okay, I have the lights off. Debbie is going to increase the light a little at a time. Here we go, open your eyes."

Slowly Michael opened her eyes. The room was an inky haze of shadows with the largest shadow directly in front of her. There was a click as the lights were turned up a notch. Now the shadows started to take form. Michael could see the small frame of Dr. Huang, Kelly sitting against the wall, and next to him, Debbie, the nurse apparently, at the light switch.

Again another click.

The shades of gray and black were changing into colors. Still muted but becoming more defined with each passing second.

"Okay, Michael, tell me what you see."

"I am seeing colors, and everything is sharp and clear. At first everything was blurred, but not now," she signed as Kelly's soft tenor filled the air with her words.

"Are there unpleasant or painful sensations?" Huang's face moved closer to Michael's.

"No."

"Good, then I'm going to turn the lights up two more notches. Here we go."

The red of Kelly's hair was bright against the thick green sweater he wore. His freckles stood out sharply on his boyish features. The gray in Dr. Huang's hair had, over the years, taken over the jet black that he had retained most of his adult life. Michael clapped her hands together. She was overjoyed that her vision had not been damaged.

"I'm glad you're happy, but before you get too enthusiastic, let's have a deeper look. Now I am going to put some drops into your eyes that will dilate your pupils. After that you will not be able to see clearly, but I'm sure Kelly here will take good care of you." The doctor, without further delay, placed two drops in each eye.

Within a few minutes, Michael's vision had become unfocused enough to make it uncomfortable to keep her eyes opened. Dr. Huang looked at her retinas, declaring them free of damage. After a few more instructions on how to wear the "extremely unfashionable sunglasses" and a promise that Michael would come back in three weeks, Michael was ready to leave.

Kelly led Michael back to his car and onto their next appointment.

"Do you wanna have an early lunch before we go to the police station?" Kelly inquired as they drove up I-10.

"No. I don't think I would be able to keep any food down. I am a nervous wreck. I don't know why I even have to do this. I don't remember a fucking thing," Michael told Kelly, trying anything not to have to go and relive the whole attack.

"I know, but them's the rules, kiddo," Kelly's voice was reassuring as Michael felt his hand cover hers.

Suddenly, Michael was terrified. Tears began to run down her cheeks. "Kelly," she said using his sign name, "K" over the heart.

"I know. Do you want me to stop?"

"Yes, and take me home," she signed through her tears, even though she knew that wasn't possible.

"The best I can do is stop at Starbucks. That's the only reprieve I can give you."

Michael agreed to that. They each ordered a large caramel-flavored coffee and sat at a small table in silence. After she had drunk half of her coffee, she told Kelly she was ready to go.

CHAPTER 7

The trip was long and quiet. Neither Michael nor Kelly spoke. Michael was afraid that if she so much as tried to have a conversation, she would fall apart, and Kelly was empathic enough to understand her need for a moment of quiet panic before they arrived at the police station.

By the time they arrived, Michael's vision was starting to come into focus. The traffic had been bumper to bumper and had cost them almost an hour to travel the thirty miles from Katy, a western suburb where Dr. Huang's office was, to the police station in the Heights.

Still, Kelly insisted that Michael take his arm as he led the way into the station. At the front desk, Kelly informed the officer that they were there to see Officer Jean Boudreaux. They were instructed to have a seat and wait but not for long.

Michael noticed the short stocky man as he headed their way. As he neared, his features came into focus. He was a dark-complexioned man with tight curls. He wasn't much taller than Michael, she assumed, maybe five-seven, five-eight. She could tell that he tried to soften his features as he neared, but somehow it only made him seem harder.

"Ms. Braun, I'm Jean Boudreaux, the officer in charge of your case. We met at the hospital, but I am sure you don't remember much," he said, his voice heavy with the sound of the Louisiana swamps. "As you requested, I have arranged for an interpreter."

Michael noticed his prolonged glance at Kelly and signed, "This is my friend Kelly Smyth-Hartman. I want him to be able to stay with me," Kelly's voice again giving her words sound.

"That's no problem, but I want to use the department's interpreter. Is that a problem?" Boudreaux asked.

Michael shook her head no.

"Okay, if you'll follow me."

Michael reached for Kelly's hand; then together, they followed the officer through the maze of the station until they entered a room used, presumably, for conferences or interrogating.

After a brief introduction to the interpreter, a woman whom Michael had used before, Boudreaux started.

"Ms. Braun, have you been able to remember anything at all since we last spoke?"

"No," Michael admitted.

"We've been able to collect very little evidence, both at the parking garage and at your house. Your attacker was very thorough, almost professional, in his ability to leave a miniscule amount of trace evidence behind. And I have to tell you this attack was personal." Boudreaux's voice was flat when he added the last statement.

"What do you mean?" Michael was stunned. She hadn't really thought about it before that very moment. It had been personal to her; it had happened to her. She didn't understand what he meant. "What do you mean?" she asked, wanting to understand how her house had been burned to the ground and how she had been attacked could be anything but personal.

"Yes, I understand where you're coming from. However, you weren't robbed or raped. You were found fully clothed although the clothes were torn. You had your purse with, by all accounts, a wallet full of cash and credit cards. Whoever did this to you"—and a file folder with the edges of photos sticking out was slid across the table to Michael—"wanted to hurt *you*."

Michael pulled the folder closer and started to open it. Kelly's hand slapped the folder close, demanding Michael's attention to be focused on him.

His eyes were wide, and a deep streak of crimson had appeared from under the collar of his sweater to spread across his face. "Michael." It was one word, but it contained so much meaning that it stilled Michael to the core.

"I have to," she said, signing to Kelly and hearing the voice of the interpreter.

"Ms. Braun has just had the bandages that have covered her eyes since the attack removed, and by now, her eyes are seeing clearly," Kelly snarled at Officer Boudreaux.

"Holy shit!" Officer Boudreaux said under his breath.

"I have to," she said again.

Kelly removed his hand.

What stared back at Michael as she opened the folder drove her to her feet and against the wall. It was her, beaten beyond recognition. She had known she had been, but these pictures were . . . She turned to face Kelly and, for the first time, caught her reflection in the two-way mirror that had been behind her.

She screamed. It was all the more powerful in its lack of sound. She crumbled to the floor as Kelly rushed to her. "I'm going to take her home now," Michael heard Kelly say as she was pulled to her feet. "If you have any other questions, you can come to the house. I'll call with the address. She's had enough for today."

Michael allowed herself to be propelled from the interrogation room to the car. She was in a daze as Kelly drove. She was vaguely aware that Kelly was talking to someone on his cell phone.

Her face, torn and swollen, covered in blood, kept staring back from the glossy photos. She had been aware that her hair had been shaved, but her attacker had chopped it off, leaving great patches of close cropped hair next to longer bloody strands. Her eyes were swollen shut by the blows or by the chemical that had been sprayed, Michael wasn't sure. She couldn't breathe. She was sure she was going to pass out, but the images just continued to play themselves over and over in her mind.

"Michael." She heard Kelly speak her name.

She turned to look at him and saw the pained expression on his face.

"Michael, we're home. Honey, you need to get out of the car and come into the house." Kelly gently pulled her out of the car.

"I'm okay," she said.

"I know, but I'm going to give you something to help you relax. Have a seat."

Michael found herself in the kitchen, sitting at the bar. "Just sit there for a moment."

Michael did as she was told, aware only in a peripheral manner as Kelly made a sandwich for each of them. As she ate, she had the feeling of watching herself. After she had finished the sandwich, Kelly handed her a glass of water and a pill, which Michael dutifully took.

The next thing she knew, Michael found herself being undressed and then redressed into her pj's and put to bed.

Somewhere Kelly's voice told her that he had given her a tranquilizer, and she would sleep most of the day and night.

"I'm not going anywhere," she heard him say as she felt his lips kiss her cheek.

CHAPTER 8

It was almost seven o'clock when Dan pulled into the garage of his condo. Kelly's car was parked behind Michael's, which meant that he was still here. Good, then maybe he wouldn't have to cook dinner.

The house was dark, and there was a distinct lack of cooking odors. He grew uncomfortable as he worked his way from the first floor to the third. On the large king-size bed, Dan noticed the top of Michael's head, but it was a noise from the study that drew his attention.

Kelly was getting up from the couch and heading his way. He had placed his finger over his lips as a signal for Dan to be quiet and motioned him to follow down the stairs. Dan followed Kelly down to the first floor and through the kitchen and into the garage, where Kelly closed the door.

He immediately flew into a fury but kept his voice to a whisper as he raged on, "That stupid mother-fucker thought it was a good idea to show our Michael some photos of her recent hospital stay. She had no idea how badly she had been beaten, but he sure as shit made sure she was brought up to speed."

Dan had only seen Kelly this incensed once before and had never hoped to experience it again, but this time, he was beginning to share the feeling.

"I have known Michael for a long time. She is the calmest and most collected person I know, and that includes your brother. She never cries, never breaks down, but she crumbled to the floor like a rag doll. I had to sedate her with something to knock her out. The shit is strong enough to keep down a horse, but she's been tossing and turning since I got her to bed."

Dan was shocked to see tears in Kelly's eyes. He wasn't a crier either. Well, except when it came to the triplets, but Dan could tell the tears were from anger, not sadness.

"Look, Kelly, you go home. Just tell me what to do, and I will stay up there. I can sleep on the couch, and if she wakes up, I'll be there. Go home and let David take care of you. You seem to have had a tough day too." Dan pulled Kelly into his arms and hugged him, gently patting his back. After a moment, Dan kissed Kelly's forehead and led him to his car. Once he was inside, Dan spoke, "I'll call David and tell him you're on your way home and ask what I need to do."

Dan stood and watched as the car backed out of the driveway and headed up the street. After the car had disappeared from view, Dan went into the house and called David.

Dan explained to David what had happened, which he already knew from the phone calls from Kelly throughout the day. He was told simply to keep an eye on Michael. If she were to wake up, just make sure she remains calm and see if she would drink some water.

He spent the next hour fixing and eating a light dinner, changing into shorts and a T-shirt, calling his boss, letting him know that he would need a personal day tomorrow, and gathered bedding for the couch.

Dan tried to read the new James Patterson book but couldn't get past the first paragraph he seemed to have been reading for the last thirty minutes. Twice he had gotten up and checked to make sure Michael was breathing since he had settled on the couch.

David had agreed to call Dan on his cell phone, which would be on "vibrate" to check on Michael. Kelly had called to make sure they were fine three times before he had to tell David to do whatever it took to get Kelly to calm down.

He laid back and willed himself to relax.

A persistent pounding brought Dan to his feet. The light of the bathroom poured into the bedroom and illuminated Michael as she pounded the wall. Dan ran to her and waited for the right moment when her arms were against her side before he encircled her in his arms.

"Michael." His voice was calm and soothing. "Michael, you're all right. Nothing here can hurt you. Michael, it's Dan. I need for you to wake up." It had become clear as Michael continued to struggle against an invisible attacker that she was not fully conscious.

"Michael."

She stilled in his arms. Dan loosened his grip and stepped back so he could look at her. She was looking up at him, her eyes glassy and clear. They shimmered with unshed tears. Dan lost his breath as he lost himself in her eyes. They were the color of violets, deep and rich, and they seemed to look right through him.

"Why?" She signed. "Why did he do this?"

Dan didn't know how to respond. She didn't give him the chance.

"He hit me and hit me and hit me!" The violence with every movement in her signs devastated Dan. He could feel the pain being inflicted each time she repeated the words.

Dan did something he would never have done under normal circumstances—he took her hands so she couldn't sign. "I don't know, Michael." He pulled her to him and carefully kissed her forehead. "I don't know"—he kissed her cheek—"but you're safe." He kissed her trembling lips. "I won't let anyone hurt you again." Dan was surprised by the savagery and sincerity in his voice.

Michael seemed to fold into Dan, and together, they moved to the bed. Dan tucked Michael in and moved to sit on the edge of the bed. Michael pulled Dan back. "Don't go," she begged.

Dan got into bed next to Michael and felt his heart rate increase as Michael moved to wrap her legs around his and bury her face in his chest. Dan could feel the hot tears as they spilled from her eyes.

He stroked her back, mindful of the wounds there. "You're safe," Dan chanted, willing himself to believe he could keep her safe.

"Don't leave," Michael signed in the air above their intertwined bodies.

"I won't."

As she quieted, Dan relaxed as well. The weight of her against him was erotic and, at the same time, familiar. The pj's she wore were thin, and her breast pressed against him. He would lay there in such sweet torture for the rest of his life, just to have her near him. She rolled over, pulling Dan with her so that she fit into the contour of his body. His arm was wrapped protectively over her. As they drifted off to sleep, Dan noticed the time on the digital clock: 10:15.

CHAPTER 9

The large antique grandfather clock that stood guard in the stately foyer chimed the quarter hours as Catfish and his wife, a petite blond woman, moved from the garage into the vast open living space. With a flick of a light switch, the combination kitchen, breakfast, and family room was lit with a soft warm glow.

They had spent the evening at Vic's on the River, a restaurant that provided an upscale and elegant dining experience. Nothing was too good for his children, and his daughter, Anna Beth, had requested a family dinner, along with several of her friends at Vic's.

Prior to the family's leaving their fashionable home, Catfish had gifted his sweet sixteen with a Mercedes SLK convertible. The previous year, his son, Nathan, received a Hummer for his sixteenth birthday.

The one thing Catfish had promised himself when as he got older, he would not do to his wife and children what his father had done to him. His family was kept separate from his other appetites.

"Ava June," Catfish continued the conversation that they had begun inside the car and had paused once inside the garage, "I know that Pastor Mason wants me to take over as head deacon, but right now, I have to finish this business in Houston before I can accept his offer."

"Well, darling," Ava June spoke from the kitchen as he poured himself a scotch, "I understand that and so does he. But we have been a pillar of Daufuskie Island Baptist Church for eleven years. Pastor Mason said he could wait another month before he would have to look for a different candidate."

"I'll accept his offer, my little Georgia Peach, but not tonight at eleven fifteen." He sipped his drink and waited for her to reply.

She did reply, and pleased with the promise she had received from her good Christian husband, she purred, "Catfish, I know you need to do some work before coming to bed, but . . . " her thick Georgian pronunciations seeming to elongate each word she pronounced.

He watched as she moved from the kitchen to where he stood. Like everything else he possessed, she was the best: good breeding, good manners, and exquisite tastes. She possessed the looks and demeanor that other men noticed. But it was Catfish this Southern beauty desired. Ava June sidled up to him, kissing him suggestively on the mouth. "Don't stay up to long."

He returned her kiss and gave her firm ass a pinch. “Oh, honey, I will make it a short and sweet as possible.”

Ava June looked up at him for a moment, her deep blue eyes holding questions and promises. “Well, Catfish, I surely hope you weren’t”—her voice dropping to a husky whisper—“talking about sex.”

Catfish laughed at her, with her. He had always had a healthy, if somewhat sedated, sexual relationship with Ava June. Unlike his trips into the seedier side of sex, his relationship with his wife was robust but not exotic.

He kissed her again and watched as she headed up the stairs. Catfish waited a few minutes, sipping his scotch before walking to the back of the kitchen, and opened a door that appeared to lead to a pantry. It was, however, an elevator that led to a turret containing his office. He closed the door behind him and entered the code that allowed him and only him to ascend the four stories to his office.

The elevator arose to the center of a twenty-foot-diameter room with large tinted windows providing him a 360-degree view of the private access to the Atlantic his Daufuskie Island subdivision provided. He stood there a moment looking to the south along the coast that led back to Savannah before walking to the wood-and-glass desk.

Scanning both his messages on the plasma screen of his laptop and the flashing indicator light of his desk phone, he noticed the caller ID on his phone and, with a sigh, picked up the receiver and dialed the Houston area phone number.

“Yes,” the Catfish barked as the other end of the line was picked up.

“You’re gonna like this,” the voice assumed.

"It had better be good. I just spent a wonderful evening with my family. I don't need your bullshit tonight."

"I wouldn't have called you, sir, unless it was important."

He hated the whiny tone of the man's voice. "Well, then, go ahead," he ordered the man as he pulled out the plush leather office chair, sat down, and lit a cigarette.

"I found her."

"IT!" Catfish roared into the line.

"Yes, sir, I found *it*." The man's placating voice whined in Catfish's ear.

"Well?"

"You know, the faggot, the one it works for? He has a brother, and it's staying with him. But the situation is even better than that. He's a detective for the West Houston/Katy police department." The man's voice laughed.

"Well now, that is something." He blew out several rings of smoke before returning back to the phone. "Okay, this makes things even better. I will fax you some instructions tonight. I'll be out Thursday night. That gives you two days to take care of everything on the list. I expect you to have everything ready when I get there. Make sure I'm not disappointed."

"Oh, no, sir! I will have everything ready before you arrive," the man added with his usual submissive tone.

"Good. Now my wife is waiting for me in bed." He hung up the phone without another word and after extinguishing the cigarette.

Catfish quickly typed up a list of requirements he would need when he returned to Houston. He had developed a coded shorthand that he had made the idiot in Houston memorize. He knew the code was necessary to ensure that if any correspondence fell into unintended hands, there would be no possible way his wishes would be understood.

Catfish did this for family, but more importantly, he did it for himself. His father had not been so careful with his appetites and indiscretions, and it had cost him not only his position in the community but ultimately his life. Catfish would not jeopardize himself like his father had, even though, for the most part Catfish's sexual behavior made his father's look like that of an innocent, starry-eyed idiot.

After the communication had been printed and faxed, Catfish returned to the first level then up the stairs to his waiting wife.

CHAPTER 10

Michael woke up to a still darkened room. Glancing at the clock on the nightstand, she saw that it was almost seven. It wasn't the darkness of the room or the rested feeling she had that had permitted her to come fully awake. It was the realization as she climbed through the layers from sleep to wakefulness that she was not alone in the bed.

Her head was pillowed on Dan's shoulder with his legs intertwined with hers. Her night shirt had traveled up, and Dan's hand had moved to cup her breast. By the rhythmic pattern of Dan's breathing, Michael knew he was still asleep. She did nothing to wake him.

It had been almost three years since she had found herself in the arms of a man. It wasn't as if Michael didn't have dates. She did, but she didn't just go to bed with anyone. Her grandmother had taught her to respect herself and that sleeping around wasn't something that anyone who respected themselves did. Michael held on to that principle. It wasn't as if she had had sex with Dan, but God, it was nice to be held.

She snuggled deeper into his body. Her movement caused Dan to turn on his side, pulling Michael with him so that they spooned. His arms tightened around Michael, bringing her more firmly against him.

Michael relaxed against him, enjoying the contact. She wasn't sure how much time had passed, but after some time, his breathing changed. Slowly, as if not to draw attention to its position, his hand moved from her breast to her stomach. He didn't pull away but moved his face so that his mouth rested above Michael's ear.

"How did you sleep?" His breath warmed her skin as he asked the question.

She managed to free her arms and hands and signed, "Great, finally."

"I was worried about you."

"Me too," Michael admitted. "It's one thing to know that you look like . . . well, like someone tried to kill you. It's another thing to actually see what you looked like only moments after it happened. I wasn't ready for what I saw."

"Boudreaux is an asshole for pulling that stunt. If I could have gotten my hands around his neck last night, I'd have given him some of his own medicine." Dan's angry words vibrated through Michael's body.

As Dan tried to disentangle himself from her, Michael reached for his arms. When she had his attention, she said, "Don't." It seemed to be the right response; he pulled her back to him configuring his body to hers.

"This wasn't my intention. I don't want you to think I am taking advantage of you. I'm not. If you tell me to back off, I will." His voice echoed in her ear with somber quality.

"I don't want you to let go. I didn't realize how much I missed waking up in someone's arms and how nice it is. That they are your arms," Michael confessed, astounded that those sentiments had flowed off her hands.

Dan laughed then kissed the top of her head and, after a moment, spoke in an amused tone. "It dawns on me that if you didn't know I was a cop, you might not know a few other important things about me."

"Such as?" Michael mused, her signs languidly articulated.

"I don't care for Chinese food but love sushi. Or I had a dog once named Clark Gable. Mother named him. Have you ever heard David say I was his baby brother?"

Michael nodded and signed yes.

"Did he tell you that I was his baby brother by ten minutes?"

Michael tried to get up. Dan held her firmly but gently down.

"You're kidding," she finally said.

"Nope."

This was really too strange, Michael thought. She had known David for so long she could draw his face by heart. She wondered if they were exactly the same. She was aware she had seen him the night before, but in her drugged and confused state, Michael was not able to remember seeing Dan's face.

"Identical or fraternal?"

"Identical."

"Weird. So are you *exactly* the same?" she teased.

"No, he's gay, I'm not. Other than that I suppose we are." Even though there was laughter in his voice, Michael could hear the serious undertone to his question when he asked, "Have you slept with my brother before?"

"Yes, I have, but not in the biblical sense. David and I have put each other to bed on many occasions in our younger days and that included undressing each other. I have seen his naked butt, and he has seen mine. However, it was only two best friends taking care of each other, nothing more."

Michael allowed her words to sink in before excitedly saying, "Okay, I am going to keep my eyes closed, but I want you to just let me do this and be quiet. It's just a little experiment. I could draw David's face in my sleep. I want to feel what you look like before I see. Does that make sense?"

"Sure," Dan said hesitantly, Michael hearing the amusement in his rich voice.

With the gracefulness of a dancer, Michael moved. She pulled Dan up to a sitting position with her legs wrapped over his and behind his back. They were so close their centers almost touched. She faced him, her eyes lightly shut.

Michael gently laid her fingers on Dan's head, feeling the texture and cut of his hair. Unhurriedly, she felt the shape of his head, then moved to his ears. Tracing the contour of each ear, she memorized him. From his ears, Michael's fingers moved to his face; there she explored the lines of his forehead and his eyebrows. She lightly drew the tips of her fingers over his eyelids, then to his cheekbones and then to his nose. With an index finger, she traced a line down the bridge to the tip, testing the flair of his nostrils.

Then she moved on to his lips.

Here she indulged herself. With her head bowed in concentration, she committed to memory the fullness of his bottom lip with its slight indention on the left corner. His mouth, slightly parted, gave Michael full access to his upper lip. It was a perfect match of its lower counterpart, framed with the stubble of an unshaved face.

A moan escaped from Dan's lips as Michael continued. He didn't move to stop her, and she didn't want to stop.

Next her hands encased his neck, feeling his beard as it too traveled down his throat. Dan's Adam's apple was not pronounced, but under the soft caressing of Michael's fingers, she felt it move. From his neck, she moved down his chest. It was covered in a thick carpet of hair. Michael wanted to continue to explore but stopped at Dan's nipples. "David's nipples are pierced," Michael commented.

She did not open her eyes but allowed a slow smile spread over her generous mouth before trailing her fingers down Dan's chest and then lower. Dan's stomach gave a shudder before her wrists were captured by two large trembling hands.

She lifted her head and opened her eyes. Dan was looking at her, looking into her. Michael felt a fire deep inside her start to come alive. His eyes moved from her eyes to her lips and back.

"God, you're beautiful."

Michael knew he was seeing past the swollen and bruised face when he said that.

"I didn't know you had such incredible eyes. Last night when I saw them, I couldn't breathe. Who are you?" he asked as he leaned in to kiss her gently on the mouth.

His lips moved from her mouth, trailing down her neck to the top of her breast, stopping above her stitches. As expertly as Michael had moved, Dan moved so that Michael was underneath him.

"I want you. I hurt for you. But I want it to be right. I want you to know that I care for you. I don't think you've had a lot of that in your life. I see that when I look into those incredible eyes of yours."

Michael rolled her eyes and with her fingers signed, "Ha-ha."

"What's that supposed to mean, ha-ha?" Dan said, releasing her wrists.

"That sounded like something from a really bad romance, 'I hurt for you . . . I see that when I look into those incredible eyes,'" Michael began in a teasing manner.

Dan moved his lips only inches from Michael's face, kissing her again. "I do, and they are," he whispered, then pressed himself into her, giving Michael clear indication of exactly how much he "hurt," how much he wanted her. Her body responded as she bowed into him. She reached up and took his head in her hands, bringing his lips back to hers. She wanted him.

"Not yet." He whispered into her mouth. "Not yet."

If she had been capable of whimpering, Michael was sure she would have. Dan reached for her hands and pulled them over her head, then ran his hands down her arms, her sides to her waist. Michael could see the conflicted emotions in his eyes, on his face. She didn't care.

CHAPTER 11

The sound of the garage door into the kitchen brought both their attention to the staircase.

"Shit," Dan whispered.

Michael thought the same.

With a carelessness that did nothing to mask the intensity of the moment that had just passed, Dan got up from the bed and moved to the couch, where Michael noticed blankets piled at the end. Gathering them up and holding them in front of his body, Dan gave Michael a crooked smile and waited for whomever it was to come up the stairs.

For her part, Michael returned to the head of the bed and, after gathering her legs so she could rest her chin on her knees, pooled the covers around her.

Kelly bounced up the stairs and came to a dead stop at the top. He looked from Michael to Dan and back to

Michael. To Michael's surprise, he didn't utter anything for a moment and then turned to Dan, asking, "How did she do last night?"

"It was rough for a while, but we made it through."

Michael watched as Kelly stared at Dan for what seemed like an eternity before turning his attention to her.

With blankets still in hand, Dan moved to the stairs. Turning back to face the bed, he said, "I'm off today. I'm going to take a shower and get dressed, then I am taking you two to Katz's Deli for breakfast." Without waiting for a response, he descended the stairs.

"Well, well, well!" Kelly said as he moved toward the bed, switching on the lamp as he sat on the edge.

He didn't say anything but looked at Michael with his eyes squinting. Michael raised an eyebrow at him. "You're here awfully early this morning," she commented. When Kelly only looked at her with one eyebrow raised almost to his hair line, she added, "What?"

Kelly cleared his throat and moved closer to Michael. "I'm here to take out your stitches," he said flatly.

Michael watched as he reached into the small bag he had brought upstairs with him. "I got you some soap that you can use in the tub. It is gentle enough so it won't hurt any areas that are still tender. Also, you can wash your hair, but use baby shampoo and don't scrub near your stitches for another week or two."

He started to get up and then sat back down.

"Okay, I say this because you are like a sister, and I love you." Michael watched as Kelly searched for words, something he never seemed to do. "Dan is a wonderful, caring man. All the great things that I love in David are there in Dan. He is a little rougher around the edges, but it makes him who he is. He needs someone wonderful and so do you."

Michael started to sign something, but Kelly held up his hand to stop her. "The sexual tension was so strong it nearly knocked me back down to the first floor when I hit the third-floor landing. And I'm a man, and I can tell when a man has a hard-on so bad he can't walk correctly, so that whole blanket thing didn't work. Look, all I'm saying is give it a chance if that's what you want. Is that what you want?"

Before Michael could answer, Kelly warded off any answers with a wave of his hands.

Michael took Kelly's outstretched hands and was pulled to her feet and led into the bathroom. She sat on the toilet seat as Kelly went about checking then removing her stitches. They were silent for an unusually long time.

Kelly announced that the stitches were out, and everything looked wonderful. He told Michael to take a shower and hurry up about it because he was hungry. Before he left, he enfolded Michael in his arms and whispered into her ear wickedly, "If he is half as well-endowed and one-fourth as passionate a lover as his brother, baby, you are in for a wonderful surprise."

With those words, Michael's hot shower became a long cold one.

CHAPTER 12

"Hey, sleepyhead," Dan's voice whispered in Michael's ear, "I have to get to work, but I brought you some coffee."

Michael opened one eye and peered up at Dan. He was dressed in a wool suit and had a fresh showered scent. His finger pointed at the large coffee mug on the bedside table.

Michael stretched under the tasseled covers, exposing a bare breast.

"Good morning to you too," Dan said as he leaned over and took the upturned tip of Michael's breast into his mouth.

Michael didn't want him to stop, knowing that was as far as he would go. Before the sheer torture of his tongue playing over her taunt nipple was about to send her over the edge, his lips moved to hers.

"I'll be home late tonight. I have to make up for the wonderful day we had together Wednesday. Yesterday just barely caught me up on paperwork, so today I want to get a head start so that I can get off early tomorrow. That way we can have most of Saturday and all of Sunday." He kissed her again and headed down the stairs.

Michael watched as he descended.

Wednesday had been a wonderful day. It had been a day like one she hadn't had in . . . maybe all her life. When she had finally come downstairs after her long cold shower, she was dressed in jeans that should have been tight but weren't. Michael had found a bra that didn't hurt her back, a classic from Victoria's Secret and added a cashmere turtleneck that hugged the ample curves of her breasts.

She covered her head with a scarf that matched the sweater and topped the look off with lip rouge, sunglasses, and Dr. Martens. She was rewarded with obscene catcalls from Kelly and a long appreciative whistle from Dan.

Their breakfast at Katz's Deli on Westheimer and Montrose Avenue had been fun and filling. While they breakfasted on bagels, cream cheese and lox, potato knishes, and blintzes topped with apples and cinnamon, Dan had decided they would spend the day at the zoo and the nearby art museums and, if they were not too tired, maybe go to watch the Houston Rockets play against the Chicago Bulls at 7:00 p.m.

He had asked Kelly to get the kids and accompany Michael and him to the zoo. Kelly declined, saying that while most of the swelling and bruising had gone down, it was still enough so that the kids would ask questions Kelly didn't feel like having to answer. Michael reluctantly agreed with Kelly, saying the kids didn't need to be worried or frightened because of her.

Dan had added, before it got too cold, they would all go—David, Kelly, the kids, Michael, and himself.

The day at the zoo had begun at eleven and had been a dream. They had both slipped easily into ASL while they discussed the animals, their dreams, politics, religion, sports, their professions, and any subject they could think of with the exception of the attack. They ate hot dogs, ice cream, and sipped fresh iced tea.

After about four hours, they headed to a local restaurant on Loop 610 South called Pappadeaux, where they dined on Cajun seafood. The meal was followed by the basketball game. Michael enjoyed the crowd more than the game and enjoyed Dan's company more than the crowd.

They left before the end of the third quarter. The Rockets were winning by a large margin, and Dan had realized that Michael was exhausted. It had been the first time since the attack, ten days before, that Michael hadn't had a nap in the middle of the day. Between the foods, the drinks, the walking around Hermann Park zoo, and the effects of the day before, Michael was ready to pass out.

Dan apologized all the way to the car and most of the way home until at a stoplight near the old Warwick Plaza, now the Hotel ZaZa, she kissed him into silence.

When they arrived home, Dan had told Michael to go up and get ready for bed. He had a few things to do. Michael went up and, after washing her face, brushing her teeth, and changing into her Pooh and Tigger pajamas, sat on the couch in the study. She was tired but didn't ever remember having such a wonderful day. She was replaying the day over in her mind when she heard Dan's voice asking her to come downstairs.

Michael found Dan waiting for her on the second-floor landing. He kissed her then said, "Kelly told me you liked to work out. Well, it just so happens I have a workout room here." He led the way into a spare bedroom that had been turned into an office with a desk and new computer along with the latest multipurpose exercise equipment. "The exercise equipment never gets used. I get enough exercise chasing the bad guys." He laughed at his own joke.

Michael looked at him. He had changed into sweatpants that had been cut off into shorts. He was shirtless and sexy. Michael followed the contours of his body with her eyes as she took in the sight of him.

"Hello," Dan said, pulling Michael against him, wrapping his arms behind her back. "If you look at me that way, I will not be able to continue to be the gentleman my mother would expect me to be."

"I think you're too much of a gentleman already," Michael told Dan, leaning into him rubbing her body against his.

She watched as he shook his head and, taking her hand, led her into his bedroom. Unlike the room where they had been sleeping, his was dark and masculine. It was probably the only room in the house Dan had furnished himself.

What shocked her was the bed. Where, for some reason, Michael had expected a large king-size bed, she discovered a queen-size instead.

She looked at Dan, raising a quizzical eyebrow.

"I don't want to lose you in the night," He answered.

Michael didn't say anything as she was led to the bed. Dan pulled the covers back and indicated that she crawl in. When she hesitated, Dan gently said, "You're safe."

Michael took a deep breath and crawled under the covers. Dan turned off the lamp and moved to the other side of the bed and joined Michael. He moved to her and took her in his arms. "I told you this morning, I was going to wait. I want you to have this a little further behind you. But"—he kissed her ear—"I want you right here so I can be here if you need me."

Michael allowed the tears to stream silently down her face. Tears she had never before seemed to shed, but now she seemed to cry at the slightest provocation.

Dan held her, nuzzled her, but made no attempt to do more. Michael was sure he had wanted more as his body betrayed him and he wasn't shy about his desire.

That was how their first real day together had begun and ended.

CHAPTER 13

Thursday had begun with Michael wakened with coffee and a kiss. Dan had explained to her what his day was possibly going to be like. He had made sure Michael had his iPhone number so she could call or he could call her if something came up.

After Dan had left, Michael went to the workout room and did a moderate workout, her first in almost two weeks. The workout was followed by a light breakfast then a shower.

She spent the rest of the morning text-messaging her insurance agent, trying to get the ball rolling so Michael could recoup the loss of her house. Also she checked with the office manager at David's office to see how long she had before she was required to return to work. Michael was pleased to discover that David had given her an extended leave of absence with pay until she was ready to get back to work.

Using her remote relay, a service that allowed her to access an interpreter via her computer's monitor and a webcam, Michael contacted Officer Boudreaux to schedule an appointment for Friday. She would be ready for her interview this time and wanted to get the whole thing behind her as soon as possible.

Next, she called Sean, her brother. Michael text-messaged Sean so he would go to his computer and get his system set up. Within a few minutes, Michael was looking at her brother's handsome face.

"Shit, Michael, you look terrible," Sean said after staring at her for a solid minute.

"Gee, thanks. You really know how to make a girl feel wonderful," Michael replied with a joking expression on her face.

The look of worry and anger on his freckled face softened. Unlike Michael, Sean could have been the poster child for the Irish tourist bureau. He was handsome, fair-complexioned, with deep green eyes and a devilish look about him. And like Michael, who was tall for a woman, five seven, Sean was tall for a man, six eleven. It was this combination that made him a success in his profession as an athlete and professional spokesperson.

"David promised me you were okay, Michael, but you don't look it."

Knowing there was no point in lying to him, Michael was honest. "It has been really hard on me. I have been crying like an idiot at the drop of a hat—"

"Duh, that's really not like you, but I suppose you deserve to cry as much and whenever the hell you want," Sean interrupted.

"Tell me. But I have a clean bill of health. My insurance claim should be taken care of in the next few weeks—"

Again, Sean interrupted, "What insurance claim?"

Michael, realizing David had only told Sean a selected amount of information, took a deep breath and confessed, "Whoever did this"—she motioned to her face—"also burned down my house."

Michael watched as the color, what little there was in Sean's face, melted away. "Jesus, Michael, why didn't you tell me before now?"

"Because I knew you would have gotten on the first plane to Houston, and we don't need the additional publicity of having you around with all this going on. You know it, and I know it. I am younger and wiser than you," she joked trying to lighten his dark mood.

He dropped his head into his hands, not looking at her.

Michael tapped the table, knowing that the microphone would pick up the signal for him to look up at her. "Sean, if I needed you, really needed you, I know you would come. Nothing could keep you from it. But aren't you guys doing really well and didn't you just sign a rather large contract with a shoe company?"

Sean gave her a look that made her laugh. "I keep tabs on you."

"Well, that's good to know." He looked away then back into the camera. "Michael, today is the twelfth. I am going to see if I can get some time off after the next few weeks.

I know I can't come around Thanksgiving, but the week before, I could get three or four days off. I'll sneak into town, and you can hide me out. What do you say?"

Michael loved the idea. They had sneaking into each other's private lives down to an art. With Sean's high visibility, it was essential to keep a low profile. "I can't wait."

They said their good-byes, each promising the other that they would keep in touch over the next few days and weeks. Michael was glad she had spoken with her brother. They, Michael, Sean, and their grandparents, kept each other grounded, safe from the past that had almost destroyed them all. They all attempted to keep their mother healthy and calm.

Before leaving for the mall to replace some of the clothes she had lost in the fire, Michael checked with the bank to make sure no unauthorized charges had been added to her credit or check card. There hadn't been, which relieved her.

The balance of the day had been filled with shopping for clothes, a chore that Michael considered a necessary evil, and a trip to the market for some staples she wanted to have in the kitchen.

When she had returned home and put away the food and clothes, Michael text-messaged Dan to inquire how his day was going and if he wanted her to fix him something to eat or would he be in too late. Dan informed her that he would be getting a hamburger or something somewhere around the station house. He inquired about her day before having to disconnect.

Michael had spent the evening doing some reading, careful to follow Dr. Huang's instructions and soaking in a somewhat steamy bubble bath.

That evening, Dan arrived back at the house around nine. When he walked into the house, he was lulled by the scent of the fireplace going and the subtle smell of a woman in the house. It was floral and woodsy at the same time. He followed the sound of the stereo to the living room, finding Michael stretched out on the couch in a pair of silk lounging pajamas eating a half pint of Blue Bell ice cream.

She looked up at him and smiled as he rounded the couch. "Did you save some for me?" he asked as he sat next to her.

Michael offered a spoonful of the creamy concoction. Dan opened his mouth and allowed her to feed him the ice cream. He followed the smooth texture of the ice cream with the even creamier taste of her mouth.

Dan was always taken aback at Michael's total surrender of herself to him. She leaned into his kiss, demanding as much from the kiss as he. Her fingers moved from his chest to his back, kneading his flesh as they went.

Dan had taken off his jacket and thrown it over one of the barstools before coming into the living room, allowing Michael freer access to his shirt as she tugged it free from his trousers. He wanted her, he hurt with the throbbing of his desire, but he would not give into her, not yet.

He pulled away, gently removing Michael's arms from his shirt and placing them on his knee. "I really mean it, Michael."

He could see the pain in her violet eyes. That was not his intent. Dan didn't ever want her to be in pain. How could he make her understand?

He took her hands, pulling her to her feet, then moved to the fireplace. Dan took off his shoes before sitting on the Oriental rug. Dan offered his hand to Michael, who accepted it and joined him on the floor.

"Michael," Dan started, "I don't want you to think that I don't want you." He leaned back so that the obvious bulge in his pants could be seen. "I do, oh god, I do. Just give it a few more days. Please," Dan begged. He had never begged for anything or for a woman in his life. He was begging now.

Michael moved to him. She threw her legs over his thighs and sat so close to him he could feel the heat of her desire.

"I will wait." The words she signed were small and close to her chest. "But only a few more days. Then I am going to make you miserable." She added as she touched him through the material of his pants.

Dan was sure she could make him suffer. Hell, she was doing it now just by being in the same room with him. Dan had a beer, Michael a glass of juice, as she was still on antibiotics, before they headed for bed.

As he had done the previous two nights, Dan slept with Michael in his arms. He didn't fall asleep immediately but waited until Michael's steady, even breathing informed him she was asleep. For the first time in a long time, Dan cried. He had been the happiest the last few weeks than he had in his all adult life. He almost wanted to kill David and Kelly for keeping this treasure of a woman from him. In fact, he was going to ask his brother tomorrow if that had been his plan all along.

Before he allowed sleep to finally take him, Michael had a nightmare. Dan soothed her with soft words and kisses until she calmed down and went back to sleep. After he had made sure she knew she was safe, he fell asleep.

CHAPTER 14

Michael got out of bed and went upstairs to where she had her things. She showered and dressed for her interview, or whatever the hell you'd call it, with Boudreaux. She had informed him that she would need an interpreter, not wanting to ask Kelly to go through this with her. She had to face this by herself.

By nine, Michael was dressed in jeans, tennis shoes, a sweatshirt, and a pair of dark shades and was out the door. She had found her purse and her keys under a pile of clothes needing to be washed. She made a mental note to do some laundry when she returned to the house.

Wednesday had been the last day for either Kelly or Rosie to come to the house. Before that, one or the other had washed her clothes. Now she was going to have to start taking care of herself. She hadn't realized how much she had missed that part of her life and how in such a short period of time had gotten used to being taken care of.

The drive was pleasant on yet another unsurprisingly warm November day in Houston. It was nice enough for Michael to lower the top on her Audi A5 after making sure that her head was covered with a stocking cap. It wasn't as if she looked bad. On the contrary, the shape of her head allowed the tightly cropped hair to give her an unusually exotic look. With the right earrings, her grandmother had once informed her, a woman could wear anything.

The police station was a new building, and with ample parking available, Michael was able to find a parking spot near the front door. After passing through security, she headed to the front desk. Handing the uniformed receptionist a note asking for directions to Jean Boudreaux's office, Michael was instructed through a maze of cubicles and located the officer's desk at what seemed to be the back of the squad house.

She found Boudreaux at his desk. "The interpreter isn't here yet, but it should be just a few minutes. He works for the department and had to come from another precinct."

Michael nodded her understanding and allowed herself to be led back to the same interrogation room she had been in three days before.

"Would you like some coffee?" he asked.

While she waited for him to return with the coffee, Michael focused her energy on what might be coming. She still couldn't remember what had happened, but maybe she would if the right questions were asked.

When Michael heard Boudreaux return, she turned to accept her coffee. It wasn't Boudreaux but Dan. Before she could say anything, Boudreaux returned.

"Good, you're here," he said as he nodded to Dan and handed Michael her coffee. "Ms. Braun, this is our interpreter, Detective Daniel Hartman. Detective, this is Ms. Braun," Boudreaux introduced. Then, as an afterthought directed to both Michael and Dan, the question, "I understand you two know each other, is this going to be a problem?"

Michael shook her head no.

"Boudreaux, before we get started, can I have a moment with Ms. Braun? I need to see if she requires any information about how the department's interpreter works," Dan lied, knowing full well Michael knew how this worked.

After Boudreaux had left the room, Dan turned to Michael. "Look, I didn't know about this until I got here. I was asked to come here as soon as I checked in this morning. It was only after I saw you that I knew. If you are uncomfortable with this, I can get a replacement from one of the agencies. It could take an hour or so, but I don't want you to be uncomfortable with this." He kept a professional distance, but Michael could see in his face that his concern was genuine.

She thought for a moment before telling him she was fine with the arrangement. Michael took a seat as Dan called in the detective and sat across from her. For his part, Boudreaux came in, took his seat, then asked, "If you are okay with Detective Hartman here, we can proceed?"

Michael nodded for him to go ahead.

"First of all, Ms. Braun, I want to apologize for Tuesday. I hadn't realized that you had had your eyes bandaged until just before you arrived here and hadn't seen the . . . um . . . results of the attack," Boudreaux started.

"Thank you," Michael signed and smiled inwardly as Dan's deep voice filled the air with her words.

"I hope you have been able to give it some thought and come up with something that could possibly help us find the person who attacked you." His manner was polite and congenial, a somewhat different approach than Tuesday's.

"I can't think of anything. It was all a surprise, it happened so fast."

"I understand. Can you recall anything at all?"

"Music. Someone had turned on some really loud rap." Michael suddenly remembered.

She watched as the detective leaned forward. "We found a car with the stereo on full blast. We think that it was used to cover up any sounds that the attacker might have made. The car was a few rows over, not far from your car."

Michael sat up, something in her conscience bubbling to the surface. "The music wasn't on when I was hit from behind."

Michael watched as Boudreaux wrote something on the pad that until then hadn't been touched.

She continued, "But I remember that right after I was sprayed in the face, the music started. I was being dragged from my car, so there must have been more than one person."

More questions. More writing.

"Did you see anyone out of place when you exited the elevator?"

Michael thought for a moment and nodded, "No. Rich Vaché was in the elevator with me. When I got out, he asked me if I wanted to go and have a drink with some of the people that worked on the same floor as I do. I told him no. I watched as the elevator went down before I headed to my car."

"We have Mr. Vaché's statement," Boudreaux commented flatly. He looked at his pad for a moment before asking, "Do you remember if the attacker said anything at any time during the attack?"

Michael looked over at Dan. His face held a neutral expression, but his eyes had a warm, reassuring cast as they returned her gaze. She wasn't sure if this had been a good idea or not, but at this point, it didn't really matter. He sat with his hands folded on the table before him waiting for her to continue. He made no comment or did anything of a personal nature that would be out of place in the situation. Michael was thankful for that. If he had been anything other than professional, she might have left the room before she thought of anything.

Her head snapped up, and she pounded her hands on the table. Both men jumped. "He kept repeating a word. He was screaming it at me, but I can't remember what it was. He said it over and over." Dan's rich voice gave her words the exact amount of anger and frustration she felt.

This time she looked directly at Dan, "Why didn't I remember that before?"

Dan voiced her signs, but Michael saw that he realized the question was directed to him.

Boudreaux went on to explain that often assault victims didn't remember the details easily, and sometimes the small details just popped into their heads. He suggested Michael keep a small notebook with her so if she remembered anything at any time, she would be able to write it down and get the information back to him.

Michael agreed.

Detective Boudreaux thanked Michael for coming in and, after reviewing his notes one last time, left the room.

Dan moved from around the table and sat next to her, taking her hand in his. "Are you okay?" he asked.

"Yeah, I think I am."

"I have to go back to Katy, but I'll check on you later."

Michael looked around and, seeing they were alone, kissed Dan, holding on to him tightly for a moment before letting go and getting to her feet. "I'll talk to you later," she said as she headed out of the room.

CHAPTER 15

Dan watched her go, amazed at her composure. She had answered the detective's questions, giving each considerable thought before answering. He saw the strength that David and Kelly had always commented about. Dan could see why they might call her fearless. He had begun to think that if she had seen her attacker, been aware of what was about to take place, there would have been one hell of a fight. But the bastard had made sure she was caught so far off guard she couldn't fight back.

Dan considered the information she'd given in the interview. It certainly was more that Boudreaux had before this morning, but he couldn't see how any of it was going to help locate Michael's attacker. Maybe, if Michael could remember what the man had been yelling at her, it would help. But he knew that she might never remember.

He left the station and headed back to his precinct. While he was stuck in traffic on I-10, his iPhone rang.

"Hartman," the voice on the other end, his boss Captain Parker, said without waiting for a reply. "I need for you to go to the Captain's Motel on South Telephone Road."

Dan wrote down the address on a pad stuck to the dashboard. "What's up?" he asked.

"Some hooker got herself tied to a bed and got left overnight. She's okay, but the officer in charge asked for you by name but wouldn't give me any information. Just that they needed you there before they can finish processing the scene." Parker disconnected the line before Dan could question him any further.

The Houston area traffic at its best was bad; at lunchtime, it was a bitch. It took thirty minutes just to go drive the distance on I-10 between the Sam Houston Tollway and 610 West where Dan had been when his captain called. Once on 610 heading south, it took another forty minutes to reach the Captain's Motel on South Telephone Road. Dan easily located the room by the four squad cars and several police officers standing outside the downstairs room of 109.

All eyes turned to Dan when he walked into the room. One plainclothes officer stood up from where he had been seated, questioning the woman, and introduced himself as Officer Abel Hernandez and asked, "You Daniel Hartman?"

The room was an average motel room, generic paintings on the wall, muted earth tones for all the fabrics. Also, because the Captain's Motel was known to rent rooms by the hour, it had a stench of stale cigarette smoke, alcohol, and the musty odor of sex.

A woman in her late forties and obviously the worse for wear sat wrapped in a tattered coat, smoking a cigarette. Her overly processed blond hair was pulled away from her face with a bright pink ponytail holder. What was left of her makeup seemed to age her by ten years. She looked over and glanced at Dan with an expression on her face as if to say, "What the hell do you want?"

After producing his shield for inspection, he addressed Hernandez, "Do you need an interpreter?"

"No, but I need for you to have a seat. Somehow you got yourself involved in this mess, and Ms. Galvan"—he indicated to the woman—"wouldn't answer any of my questions until you showed up." Hernandez seemed pissed that he had to have some detective he didn't even know around. Dan could tell his presence wasn't appreciated in the least.

Dan took a chair and kept his mouth shut. He didn't want to step on this guy's toes. Cops, including himself, were notoriously protective of their cases.

"Okay, Ms. Galvan, will you answer my questions now?" Hernandez asked.

"Are you Daniel Hartman?" the woman asked. Her voice was hoarse and rough from years of smoke and abuse. She looked at Dan, not at Officer Hernandez.

"Yes, ma'am, I am."

"I have a message for you, then I will answer your questions," she said to Dan then to Hernandez. "Maybe what I have to say to him will help you. I don't know much.

I was blindfolded, and I never saw the man. He wore gloves, you know, the kind that doctors wear. He kept me here for two days, memorizing this shit. I had to repeat everything that fucker said. He told me I had to get it right. I will too. He told me if I repeated everything, just like he told me, I would get $3,000. I believe him 'cause I gave him my account number and he let me call the bank and check to make sure the money was there and it was."

Galvan seemed to be on a roll. Officer Hernandez asked for and received the account number Galvan had mentioned and took more notes as Dan sat and listened. Whatever she said to him, the officer would need for his report. Dan really didn't think that this woman had anything to say that he needed to hear, but hey, this was his job.

"Go on, Ms. Galvan, you're doing great," Dan said, encouragingly using his calmest tone.

"Anyway, he had an accent. Not like some foreigner, but really Southern, not Texan! He told me to tell you, you won't find anything, he made sure of it, even vacuumed the room before he left." Ms. Galvan paused to put out one cigarette, light another, and sip some coffee in a Styrofoam cup before continuing. "He didn't hurt me, none. Just tied me to the bed, but I could get up and get something to drink and pee if I had too. He was really polite, ya know. Never talked dirty or none of that shit."

She took a deep breath, coughed, and looked right at Dan. "Here goes!"

Dan watched as she closed her eyes and took a deep breath before repeating the words she had been made to mesmerize. "Beware the Abomination. It lies," she recited, "and it will steal your soul. Beware the Abomination. It shows a beautiful face, but it is true evil. Beware the Abomination. It has already touched you, Detective Daniel Hartman. If you are not careful, it will destroy you. It may already be too late."

It was a shock to hear his name. Shit, this was freaky! Dan wanted her to stop but knew she would have to finish before he could say anything. He would have to defer to Hernandez. This wasn't his case.

"Beware the Abomination. It has destroyed lives already. You have been warned and will be warned again." She opened her eyes and looked at Dan. "That's it. But if you have questions, he said you'd have questions, you can ask. He gave me the answers to some of the questions you might ask. I'll answer if I can. If not . . . " She shrugged her shoulder.

Dan looked at Hernandez, who nodded his go ahead.

"You did well, Ms. Galvan. I am sure you earned your money." Dan tried to keep the sarcasm out of his voice. "What is the Abomination?"

"The Abomination is the Antichrist. It is Satan here on earth," Ms. Galvan said as if she was quoting from a flipchart.

That sure as hell didn't clear anything up.

"Why me?"

Again, Ms. Galvan, as she had done before, closed her eyes and quoted, "Because your soul is in jeopardy. The Abomination has already touched you. You do not know it, but you must be saved, if possible."

"Saved from what?"

"From certain death of the soul and body," she told him matter-of-factly.

"Is he, the man who tied you up and had you memorizing all this information, going to kill me?"

Ms. Galvan quoted, "It is not in his nature to kill the innocent, but if you become so entangled with the Abomination that you cannot be separated when it is killed, you might also be a victim. He will kill you, but as a Christian, your soul will be saved. To save your soul, your flesh would have to be removed from the evil."

This was truly outlandish. Dan didn't have the heart to tell her he was Jewish and his soul was just fine. He glanced at Hernandez who was taking all this in. The other officers in the room were looking from the woman to Dan, not knowing whether to laugh out loud or to shit their pants. Dan could see the confusion on each of their faces.

"Who is the Abomination?"

"That you must learn yourself, only when you find the true nature of the Abomination can it be destroyed."

"Is it a man or a woman?"

"It is an Abomination! He really screamed this part. He was pissed," Galvan added.

"Why are you the one giving this information to me and not the individual who provided all this information?" Dan was getting tired of this game. He also realized that the woman was only feeding to him what she had been fed. Sooner or later, Dan would ask a question she hadn't been prepped for, and this would come to an end. Either way, it wasn't his problem.

"He is praying and preparing to remove the Abomination from this earth."

"Where is this Abomination?"

"It is in your heart. It is in your mind. It destroys the people that you know. It is here now."

"Are you saying that it is in the hearts and minds of the people of the earth?"

"No, Daniel Hartman, it is in your heart and mind."

What the hell was he supposed to say to that? Not having a clue, he asked, "When is this Abomination going to die?"

Ms. Galvan laughed excitedly. "Oh, he was really specific about this. It got him mad. He said he had been waiting to kill this, whatever the hell it is, since it was born on this earth. He said he had waited almost all his life, and when he killed it, it would really suffer. I don't know who or what this person is, but shitfire, he hates it." The woman got up and stretched. "Can I go now?" she asked Hernandez.

Just like that, this bizarre scene had ended. Dan thanked Ms. Galvan and walked out of the room with Officer Hernandez. "What do you need from me?" Dan asked.

"I know where I can find you if I need you, but this is going to have to go straight to my captain and to yours. I haven't got a friggin' idea what to do with all this . . . stuff," Hernandez said, sounding as confused as Dan.

"Yeah, well, if I get any idea what the hell she was talking about, I'll let you know."

Officer Hernandez handed Dan his card, thanked him for his help, and returned to the room and the waiting Ms. Galvan.

CHAPTER 16

Dan was hit with four different things at once as soon as he arrived at the station house. He spent the next six hours chasing leads, following up with his partners, and catching up on paperwork he had thought he had finished but had been kicked back to his desk. Before he realized it, it was almost nine. He reached for his iPhone and texted Michael.

She texted back she had already eaten. She had assumed he had gotten busy and didn't want to bother him. Dan asked how she was doing, to which she responded that she felt great and it was good to have that interview behind her. She had spent the day finishing up some loose ends with regard to her house and was waiting for him to get home.

Dan smiled to himself as he put his phone back in his pocket. He couldn't wait to get home either. It amused him to think two weeks ago he could have cared less when he got home; it had always been a place to shower, change clothes, sleep. Now he wanted to do his job, well, then get home . . . to Michael.

"That's a hell of a goofy smile on that ugly face of yours," Mark Carson, Dan's sometime partner, said.

Dan looked up from his desk top and found Carson sitting on the corner of his desk. "My smile has character," Dan said.

"That is a 'woman on your mind' kinda smile," Carson observed.

"Well, unlike you, I might just have a woman on my mind that puts a goofy smile on my face." Dan stood up and, checking around to make sure he wasn't forgetting anything, slapped Carson on the arm. "And I need to get home to her."

As he walked out the door, he heard Carson offer an obscene comment that had Dan laughing all the way to his car.

He made several stops on the way home. He ordered a small pizza from the corner pizzeria to pick up, stopped at the grocery store to pick up some flowers for Michael, and a six-pack of beer.

Michael was not downstairs when he came in through the kitchen. The stereo was on and the fireplace going in the living room. Dan put the beer in the refrigerator and the pizza on the counter and took the dozen roses with him. He found her in the office on the computer. She had her back to the door and didn't know he was standing there. She was using the video relay and was having a conversation.

Dan stood there and watched her. The bruising had almost dissipated from her delicate skin. There was still some swelling, but nothing to draw attention to. Her head was covered now with a thick, if short carpet of rich ebony hair. Dan couldn't see her face; he didn't need to, and he could call it up at any given moment and look at Michael's beauty.

Michael turned around in her chair, and the video monitor went blank.

"Sorry to interrupt. I just got home and wanted to give you these." Dan presented the roses as an explanation for his standing and watching her.

"You didn't interrupt. I was just finishing up with my brother. He told me to thank you for taking such good care of me." She stepped forward and took the flowers from Dan.

Dan pulled her into his arms and kissed her passionately. He heard the flowers fall to the floor, and Michael's arms came up around his neck. Dan's hands were trailing down her back and found their way to the full curve of her buttocks. He moaned inside the kiss.

"I hope you didn't tell him exactly how I was taking care of you or how I was planning on continuing with your care," he said into Michael's ear as his kiss moved from her mouth to her neck.

Michael laughed silently. Dan stopped his caress and pulled away to look at her. "When you laugh, it is so different."

Michael looked up at him but signed nothing.

"There is no sound but breath, yet somehow, it seems to me to be musical. I know it's strange. It touches me so deep down."

Michael stepped into him again, and this time, it was her who started the kiss.

Later as they lay in bed, Dan realized what it was that hurt. For the first time in his life he was truly in love. He tried to rationalize his feelings; he had only known her for a little more than two weeks. Yet some other less rational part of his brain said, "No, you have known her for years, just never met." He had no idea if she was some psycho. But then again, David and Kelly had made her the triplets' version of a Jewish godmother, so she must be a loving, caring, and safe person.

This internal dialogue went on for what seemed like hours before Dan came to a conclusion. He loved Michael. He didn't give a shit how irrational it was; he knew for a fact he found the woman with whom he wanted to spend the rest of his life.

Tomorrow, he would make love to her. He had put her off. No matter how much she had teased and pleaded, he had refused. Dan now realized it was not for her, like he had told Michael, but for him that he had delayed their lovemaking. Dan knew it had been the defense he had against falling so deep he would never climb out or ever want to.

He pulled her to him, and she reconfigured herself to him. In her sleep, she kissed his shoulder, slid her slender arm over his stomach, and sealed his fate.

CHAPTER 17

Saturday morning, Michael woke to a note on Dan's pillow.

Good morning, beautiful,

I should be finished with work between 5:00 and 6:00 tonight. I would like to take you out. It's a pub, a blue jeans, sweatshirt kind of place. I would like some of my friends to meet you. If you don't want to, just let me know. Text me if you need anything.

Love,
Dan

Michael stared at the last line of the note, "Love, Dan." She reread the note before hopping out of bed and doing a jig into the bathroom. Her jig came to an abrupt stop several feet on to the tile. She wondered if it was just an expression. Men don't just put down the *L* word unless the mean it or they want something. She already knew he wanted her, though he sure as hell was resisting. She wanted him too; she had made no secret about that fact.

Oh, she needed to have lunch with her best confidant, but that was David. The idea of talking to David about Dan was gross. She might have discussed her other lovers with David, but Dan and David were so identical; it would be like discussing sex with him. Yuck! Then there was Sean, who was out because, of course, he was her brother. Double yuck! That left Kelly. Michael didn't want to think that Kelly was her last choice in her life because he wasn't. However, in the pecking order of people she talked to most of the time, David and Kelly were even. This situation was a bit different than those in the past.

She left the bathroom and headed for her iPhone. Before texting, Michael checked the time. Finding it almost nine, she texted Kelly.

It took some doing, but Kelly was able to get a sitter so they could have lunch at a Greek restaurant just off 610 at San Felipe. Over a Greek salad, Michael slid the note to Kelly. "See right there," she indicated the bottom of the note.

Kelly took a bite of salad while he scanned the note. He slid it back to Michael and sipped on his iced tea thoughtfully.

"Well?"

"I'm thinking and eating." Kelly had switched over to ASL.

This was something that David, Kelly, Sean, and now Dan did when having a conversation with Michael. It was easier to converse in one language than in two, and since Michael could only use one, naturally everyone was comfortable with ASL.

"I need your help." Michael's signs had moved closer to her chest and had become smaller, the ASL version of a whisper. "He wants to take me out, you saw the note, to meet his friends. I want to blow his mind and then later melt his pants off."

Kelly nearly choked on his bite of pita bread.

"I need some help shopping for the perfect pair of jeans and eye-popping sweater. When I walk into that bar, I want the paint to melt. You have to be my man gauge." She smiled sweetly at Kelly.

The entrées were served before Kelly could make a comment. But as soon as the waiter had left the table, Kelly said, "Look, I can tell you what I think looks good, but if you want my opinion on how to seduce a straight man, we might be in trouble. But don't worry, I know just the person to help. You know Giovanni?"

"The hairdresser?"

"That's the one, he can help and tell you if your outfit will work."

Michael shook her head. "But he's a hairdresser."

"Dear, not all male hairdressers are gay. I know for a fact, Giovanni isn't gay. The whole hairdresser gig is his way of picking up women. They love his accent. Who could blame them? I love his accent," Kelly confessed, his hands fluttering over his heart.

While Michael ate her lunch, Kelly called the hairdresser in question. He agreed to meet Kelly and Michael at his Galleria Salon at two, where he and her American Express would dress her to accomplish her mission.

At 3:56, Michael had been dressed from head to toe "to kill," as both Kelly and Giovanni put it. After learning the reason for the shopping spree, Giovanni insisted Michael come back to his salon, where he would get his makeup artist to do her face.

It didn't start or stop there. Michael and Kelly both had a full spa treatment: facials, pedicures, and manicures. Giovanni, having noticed that Michael's bellybutton was pierced, had brought a ring with a violet stone, "to match your eyes," he had told her in his sexy Italian accent.

Sometime in the midst of all the shopping and beauty treatments, Michael had texted Dan and told him that she was spending the day away from the house with Kelly, taking care of some things and would meet him at the pub at six. He gave her the address and told her to come ready for a nice, relaxing evening.

Michael had Kelly agree that before he went home, he would go by the condo in Montrose and do a bit of prep work for her. Nothing too fancy or exotic, just so when they arrived back at the house, they would have a nice place to fall into.

Giovanni's salon was roughly a thirty-minute drive from the address that Dan had given Michael. Kelly and he had insisted she dress at the salon so they could have a final inspection.

When Michael stepped out from behind the curtin, Kelly burst into applause and laughed, "Oh, he is a goner!"

Giovanni, for his part, folded her into his arms and whispered in her ear, his thick Italian accent pouring sensually over her, "I am so hard for you, yet I know I cannot have you. This is okay, because I know there is one very lucky man. I mean that in two ways. But when you become bored with him, come find me." He finished off with a kiss to both her cheeks and her glossed lips and added a very Italian pinch on the bottom for good measure.

Michael took a deep breath and headed out to her car. She threw her clothes in the trunk and slipped her driver's license, a tube of lip gloss, a small compact, and a box of Tic Tacs into a compact purse Giovanni had insisted she needed and headed off to meet Dan.

CHAPTER 18

Dan glanced at his watch. It was already 6:10, but the Houston traffic was shitty on its best day, so he wasn't worried, yet. Carson was sitting next to him at the bar at the back of the pub, along with Brown, Garcia, Danton, and Wells. All these men were men he had partnered with on and off for the last ten years. They were his friends. The bar itself was packed with maybe forty or fifty police officers or their girlfriends, wives, boyfriends, etc. The bar, O'Brian's, had several pool tables, dartboards, and a small, inadequate dance floor. Its tables were spread out so one could either sit in a large crowd or an intimate corner.

Carson was discussing his last call of the evening before he had left the station house. It was basic bullshit, but they listened, making occasional comments over their beers. It was their way of blowing off steam, releasing the pressure and stresses that could make a cop's life hell.

"Holy crap!" Garcia exclaimed, "Would you look at that!"

All eyes turned to the door as the tall woman walked into the bar; its occupants seemed to quiet down. Dan just sought to catch his breath.

Michael stood in the doorway, scanning the room. When she found Dan, she started moving toward him. She took her time walking in slow measured steps, looking every bit a runway model.

"Boy, what I could do with something like that," Carson commented.

Michael was dressed in black pants, slim and snug, that rode low on her hips. A sweater, black with a low V cut, a hemline that stopped several inches above her navel, was sculpted onto her; the top of her breasts rose and fell as she breathed. Her makeup was artistically applied to bring out the exotic curves and contours of her exquisite face. And her eyes, even across the smoky bar, were bright with their unusual violet color.

As she moved through the crowd, men moved to let her pass, following her with their eyes as she did so. Dan swiveled the barstool around to face her.

Garcia said, "Shit, she's heading this way," and proceeded to brush his fingers through his thinning hair.

To Dan, she was simply the most beautiful thing he had ever seen. As she stopped several feet from the crowd where Dan sat, he noticed the stone in her navel, obviously there to match her eyes, which winked at him. Jesus, that was sexy.

Carson said, "Hello," and the rest of the men followed suit. Dan kept his mouth shut but signed, "You are breathtaking," so that only Michael could see.

She gifted him with a smile and moved into him, spreading his legs with her knees and sliding her arms behind his back. With all eyes watching them, she kissed him. Her tongue slid between his lips and demanded a taste. He answered. It was intense and brief, and it was Michael who ended it.

She stepped away and signed, "Aren't you going to introduce me to your friends?"

Dan looked at the people in the bar, half of whom had returned to whatever they were doing, while the other half watched him and Michael with questioning faces.

"Gentlemen, I would like you to meet my girlfriend, Michael Braun," Dan addressed the men sitting next to him. He, in turn, introduced the men by name to Michael, who extended a well-manicured hand to each.

After the introductions were finished, Michael requested a glass of wine. She was off the antibiotics now for two days and was ready for something to drink, she had told Dan.

Dan ordered her a drink, and they moved to a table. They were joined by his buddies. Food was ordered, and they settled in.

"So where did you meet this ugly bastard?" Carson asked.

Dan watched as Michael held up a finger, motioning Carson to wait, and turned to him. "I don't want you to have to function as my interpreter. I want you to have fun and enjoy yourself, these are your friends." Her face told him that she was worried.

Dan reached over and kissed her; he wanted more, but for now, he would take her kiss. Speaking over his shoulder, he said, "She was literally dropped into my lap, or should I say, my house. Michael is a friend of my brother's. She needed a place to stay, and David offered my place. Lucky for me I have enough room."

"Yeah, I'll say," Danton replied.

"I have known about and have heard about Dan for over eleven years, just never met," Michael signed, and Dan interpreted for her.

"You never met in eleven years?" Carson asked.

Michael shook her head.

Dan said, "I actually saw her once but didn't know who she was."

"That's how I met my wife," Garcia began. "I saw her at a party of my brother's. We had three dates and"—he snapped his fingers—"like that we were married, wasn't even pregnant. Both our families thought she was pregnant, but it was three years before the first was born. Now we've been married for almost thirty years."

"You need to go home, Garcia. I can hear your lovely wife yelling your name," Danton teased.

They all laughed, even Garcia.

Throughout the night, Dan kept his hand on Michael's thigh. They touched each other reassuringly while conversations, food, and drink carried them through the evening.

About nine thirty, Michael told Dan she was ready to go home. She had had a good time and spent another thirty minutes thanking his friends for a nice evening. Dan watched as each of his friends said his good-byes, amused that they all had behaved like gentlemen. She kissed each on the cheek, and Dan was surprised that such a simple contact between Michael and these men fired a surprising feeling of jealousy.

"Are you feeling all right?" Dan asked Michael as he walked her to the door, stopping several times to make introductions.

"I am wonderful," Michael told him. "I just have other plans for us this evening that can't be done here." She wiggled her brows at him and kissed the side of his mouth.

"Oh!" Dan feigned surprise. He had already told the guys he was going to make sure Michael got to her car and would come back in to settle the tab. Now he wished he had paid up before and mentioned that fact to Michael.

"Don't worry. I'll be waiting for you at the house."

Dan took the keys from Michael and opened the door for her. To his surprise, she maneuvered him against the car and rubbed her hands up his chest. He could feel the heat as she pressed herself against him seductively.

"If you don't stop, I won't be able to go back in for some time. The longer it takes here, the longer for me to get home," he warned her.

"Good thinking!" Michael conceded as she pushed away from him and got into her car. "I'll be waiting."

Dan stood in the street as she started her car and pulled away. He watched her car go down the street until the tail lights of her Audi disappeared around a corner. Drawing in a ragged breath, Dan checked himself. He didn't want to look like a randy high schooler when he went back in to pay the tab.

All the men were staring at him as he walked back to the table.

Carson was the first to speak, "Does she have a sister?"

"I'd keep that one if I were you," Garcia added.

Danton, not being one to be left out of a conversation, added, "I want to know how the hell some poor slob like you ended up with something so exotic. You don't deserve her"—he broke out laughing—"but I do."

They all laughed at that. Even Dan did, but his laughter was not as congenial as theirs.

It took Dan twenty minutes of good-natured ribbing before he was able to get on the road.

CHAPTER 19

When he finally arrived home, Dan found the first floor empty. Jazz drifted down from upstairs. He threw his jacket and tie, which had been removed at the pub, over the back of one of the barstools and headed up the stairs.

On the second floor, his floor, he found it as dark as the first. The music and light was coming from the master suite on the third floor. Dan didn't care where he had to go as long as Michael was there waiting for him.

And she was.

As he topped the stairs, Michael moved out of the shadows. She was still dressed in the clothes she had worn at the pub; the only thing missing, Dan noticed, were her shoes. He moved toward her, stopping as she held up her hand. She didn't sign anything but moved with a speed that surprised him.

Dan found himself pinned to the wall, Michael's hands working at the buttons on his shirt. When he reached up to help, she slapped his hands away.

With a silent smile, Michael shook her head. The message was clear. She was in control.

Dan could think of no reason not to let her be.

She worked for a few seconds before stopping and looking him in the eyes. Her eyes were intense, her pupils dilated. There was color in her face that was not normally there. She hungrily reached up and drew Dan's mouth to her. Dan was caught up in the hunger Michael was feeling.

Dan reached up and jerked his shirt open, buttons flying everywhere. He grinned, thinking if someone had told him he would have ripped his shirt off before tonight, he would have thought them crazy.

He took Michael and moved her so she was against the wall. He kissed her neck. She reached for him with her hands. He decided he wanted to control the situation, at least the first time. He gently took both her wrists and, with one hand, held them over her head.

With the other hand, Dan undid the buttons on her pants, then slowly lowered the zipper. He worked them down over her hips and watched as she stepped out of them and kicked them away. Dan was rewarded with the sight of dangerously black lace panties. He cupped her with his hand and began working on her breast. Through her sweater, with his mouth, he concentrated on her other breast.

When her knees buckled, Dan stopped his caresses only long enough to pick her up and move her to the bed.

He watched as she struggled with her sweater. As she was about to undo the bra that matched her delicate panties, he stopped her.

"Not yet."

He watched as her hands stilled, then moved to undo his pants. He allowed her only to unbutton and unzip but moved away so she couldn't finish what she had begun. He wasn't ready. Dan slowly lowered himself over her. The taste of her skin was warm and musky. He traced his tongue over her breast. When he came to the place that had been stitched, Dan kissed it.

"I don't want to hurt you," he said, as he moved his fingers over Michael's face the way she had done to him days before. "You'll tell me if I am hurting you?"

Michael nodded.

Dan started to unsnap her bra when he noticed tears in her eyes.

He stopped cold. "Honey, what's wrong?" Dan was afraid that already something he had done had hurt her.

"It's been a while," Michael confessed, not looking at Dan.

Taking her chin in his fingers, he moved her head so she was looking at him. He leaned down and kissed the tears out of her eyes.

"It's all right."

"No, I mean, it's been over four years since I have been with anyone."

Dan rolled off her and pulled her up. He had never known anyone who hadn't had sex for four years, an adult anyway. "Really?"

Michael looked away from him.

Dan moved around so she had to look at him in the face. "Michael, why are you bothered by this?"

She didn't answer him at first. She looked at him as if measuring him. Behind the sexual passion that burned in her violet eyes was fear. It angered Dan to think she was afraid of him and asked her if she was.

The tears came again, rolling down her flushed cheeks. Dan watched as she seemed to pull herself together and steeled herself against whatever demon she was fighting.

"Before, the guy I dated wasn't very nice. When we broke up, he told me I was the worst piece of ass he had ever had. He told me to do the next man in my life a favor and don't bother. I'm afraid that maybe he was right. I don't want to disappoint you."

The lousy son of a bitch! If he could get his name, he thought he might shoot the bastard. Dan knew how bad it felt when a relationship ended, but he never tried to make the woman feel like a loser because it ended. He knew this was what had happened.

"Michael," he said as he took her in his arms, "there is nothing you can do to disappoint me. I know just by having spent the time with you as I have that you are a passionate woman. Don't let some asshole make you believe otherwise."

"I love you," Dan heard himself say, "and when you love someone and when you make love to someone, there is no room for disappointment."

He kissed her again, then looking around at the nightstand, let go a curse.

"What's wrong?" Michael asked, fear again appearing in her violet eyes.

"I don't have a condom," he told her with a sigh in his voice.

Again, Michael looked away. "I can't get pregnant. I am clean."

Trying to move the mood away from the darkness, Dan laughed and said, "Same for me. I can't get pregnant, and I don't have any communicable disease. My brother, the doctor, has good drugs."

Michael looked up at him and smiled.

It was enough.

Dan finished undressing, keeping his eyes on Michael's face. Her eyes widened when he removed his boxer briefs. That put a smile on Dan's face. He reached over and removed the lacy garments that covered her and began to show her just how wonderful a lover she could be.

Dan started at her inner thigh, moving slowly with his tongue to the center of her core. When he finally tasted her, she was hot and wet. He ran the tip of his tongue over the folds and found the spot that seemed to drive her mad.

She reached down and wrapped her fingers in his hair. Dan, with a palm open, moved his hand up her flat stomach, discovering again her pierced navel. He continued until he reached her breast and explored the taut nipples.

As her breath quickened, Dan replaced his mouth with his free hand. While he worked the responsive flesh between her legs with his hand, his mouth ravished her.

She moved under him. Her hands pushed and pulled at his chest. Dan looked down as silent moans escaped from

Michael's opened mouth. He could see in her face, in her movements, she was at the edge. He continued to stoke, to knead, until her body went rigid, her hips thrust up against his hand.

Michael's hands slapped at the side of the bed, gripping and tugging at the sheets. Her head moved from side to side until Dan took her mouth with his. She kissed him deeply, still writhing with the intensity of her orgasm.

Dan was not finished. He slid down her again, tasting her, relishing in her heat. He slid two fingers inside of her, finding her hot, wet, and tight, oh so tight.

He couldn't wait.

He lifted himself up and looked at her. "If I hurt you—"

Michael's hand moved to cover his mouth. "I love you," she mouthed the words.

Dan slid his throbbing tip against her. She parted for him; he moved deeper. She was tight, and despite the fact he wanted to impale her with a quick thrust, he slowly stroked a bit in, then out, then deeper. With each movement, he felt as if he was going to explode but controlled himself. This was for Michael; she deserved this.

Michael began to get impatient with his slowness. Dan felt Michael move against him as his hips plunged forward, causing him to go deeper. With each movement, they began to get lost. As he moved faster, deeper, and harder, his movements were matched.

She was so tight, he was sure that he was tearing her apart, but she looked at him with a hunger that frightened him. He could see his own passion reflected back at him.

Again, Michael's body tensed, the muscles tightening their grip on Dan, each wave stroking tighter, driving him over. He yelled her name as he came. It was intense and continued for longer than Dan could remember. He was spent as he lowered his still quivering body over Michael's.

"I don't know, but I have to say I have never ever felt like that in my life," Dan said between ragged breaths. "If you were any better, I would be dead."

Dan felt Michael kiss his shoulder. After a few minutes, he moved off her and laid next to her so he could see her face.

"You're beautiful."

She looked at him.

"Did I hurt you?"

She touched his cheek and ran her thumb over his lips.

"Aren't you going to say anything?"

Dan waited, his hand trailing along the skin of her back, her waist.

Michael moved away from Dan and smiled. "I don't think I am going to be able to move."

"That's okay. I'll carry you wherever you need to go." Dan meant it, he would.

They curled up and fell asleep in each other's arms, each dreaming separate dreams.

Dan dreamed of a monster, the Abomination that was eating his soul.

Michael dreamed of a monster, a killer, which was chasing her into a dark tunnel.

CHAPTER 20

Michael got out of bed and went into the bathroom. She looked at her face in the mirror and grimaced. She knew better than to sleep in makeup. She washed her face, removing the makeup and mascara. She brushed her teeth and applied moisturizer. She ran her hands over her stubble-covered head and headed back to bed. Dan was still sleeping. As much as he had worked her over last night, he probably could use all the sleep he could get.

Michael had slept with other men before, not many, but enough to know last night was something she had never felt before. Kelly had been right; she had had a wonderful surprise, several in fact.

The clock on the nightstand said six thirty. She had had six hours of sleep, but curling up next to Dan was worth being lazy for the day. As she crawled back into bed, she was greeted with Dan's smiling face.

“Good morning, handsome,” she signed.

“It is a good morning when I get to wake up next to you naked in my bed,” Dan told her as he stretched.

“This is my bed,” Michael corrected.

“Then I suppose I have to leave.” Dan started to roll out of bed; Michael tackled him before he could reach the end of the king-size bed.

“So you like it rough. I like it as well as the next guy, but, my dear, I really need to go pee, and your elbow is on my bladder,” Dan informed the laughing Michael.

“Sorry.” She let Dan up and watched as his naked backside disappeared into the bathroom. Like her, he did more than use the toilet.

Michael lay back in bed and listened to the water running in the sink.

“I don’t have to work today, do you have something you want to do?” Dan yelled at her from the bathroom. She knew there was no way to answer him until he came back to bed, so she patiently waited.

When he had finished in the bathroom and returned to bed, Michael kissed him. His mouth tasted of peppermint, his face still damp from washing. Dan wrapped himself around her and repeated his question.

“I have a few things in mind,” Michael said as she snaked her hand between Dan’s legs and found him already hard.

“I had the same idea,” Dan said as he rolled Michael on her back.

She shook her head no and, with some effort, got him on his back. She straddled him, feeling his hardness under her. Moving in a circular motion, Michael watched the play of sensations wash over Dan's face. She took her nails and lightly dragged them down Dan's chest, following the swirl of hair as it passed his navel.

As Michael's hands moved farther down Dan's body, she moved between his legs and off the end of the bed. From there, Michael began working a little magic of her own with her tongue.

She worked her way up the inside of Dan's thigh. He moaned and reached for her. Michael slapped his hands away. She was going to do to him what he had done to her the night before. As her tongue reached his sacs, she teased each one then made her way to his shaft. With each flick of her tongue, Dan caught his breath and allowed noises to escape from his lips.

Michael took him into her mouth and began to please him. She used her hands to help stroke and tease.

"Stop," Dan begged, trying to move Michael up.

She refused, concentrating on how, with each movement of her hands and mouth, Dan began to tense.

"Oh god," he yelled, this time freeing himself from Michael.

She allowed him to thrust into her with quick hard strokes. Yet she had worked him so close to climax, it was only seconds before Dan threw his head back and allowed a deep moan to leave his mouth.

For her part, Michael tightened herself around Dan, squeezing him dry. She smiled up at him just before he melted down onto her.

Sometime around noon, Dan got up and ordered a pizza for delivery. When he disappeared downstairs to put on some clothes and get ready to greet the pizza guy, Michael went into the outsized master bath and started filling the large spa tub with water. Kelly had told her how to operate the mechanics, including the temperature control and pressure for the jets.

While the spa/tub was filling, Michael spent a few minutes gathering up the clothes they had strewn about the night before. She put away all the clothes except for Dan's dress shirt, which she put on. By the time the pizza had been delivered and Dan had returned upstairs with pizza boxes, paper towels and bottles of water in hand, the room had been put into order; the spa was filled and waiting.

They ate sitting cross-legged on the bed. Together, they devoured two large supreme pizzas and two twenty-four-ounce bottles of water each.

"Wow," Dan commented as he closed the box lids, "perfect lovemaking really gives you a good appetite."

Michael laughed. "Something did. Maybe it was just having a good night's sleep."

That flippant response garnered her retaliation. Dan reached across the small space that separated them and pulled Michael to him. Michael, knowing that David was extremely ticklish, tested to see if his brother was equally so and was rewarded with an immediate answer. Quickly the situation was reversed, and Dan was on the offensive.

The impromptu wrestling match lasted for several minutes until they were laughing so hard they had to stop to breathe. After a moment to catch her breath, Michael took Dan by the hand and took him into the bathroom and the waiting spa. Without hesitation, they both removed what few garments they wore and sank into the inviting water.

Michael relaxed in the hot bubbling water of the spa. Dan carelessly rubbed his hand up and down her calf, himself appearing as relaxed as she was. The stereo that Michael had forgotten to turn off was still quietly playing in the background.

Dan's voice seemed to drift across the water when he asked, "How are you feeling?"

"Like I've died and gone to heaven," Michael admitted in slow leisurely signs.

"No. I mean that's great, but what I meant was since two weeks or so, how are you feeling?"

Michael sat up in the spa and looked at Dan. His look was one of consternation. He wanted to know, Michael surmised, if she was healing. She felt good; working out now on the exercise equipment seemed to make her recover quicker. She told Dan this.

She watched as he looked at her a moment, seeing the indecision on his face.

"Are you feeling safe?"

Michael looked down at the water. She felt as safe as she ever had. She had always felt as if she had to look over her shoulder; that was nothing new. But did she feel—

"What do you mean?" she asked, knowing full well what Dan was asking but wanted the time to contemplate any answer she might give.

Dan moved around to her. When he was closer to her, he moved behind her and slipped his arms around her waist, clasping them in front of her stomach. Michael laid her head back on his shoulder and waited.

"I mean, do you feel as if whoever did this is waiting for you?"

Michael wanted to say yes but said instead, "No, I don't think that. If I did, I would lock myself up. So no, if the bastard is out there, he's out there."

She felt Dan take a deep breath. She wasn't sure if he liked her answer, but that wasn't her problem.

"Can I ask you a question?" he asked after several minutes of silence.

Michael had decided to be as honest as possible and nodded, bracing herself for his question.

"What happened to your back?"

"Do you want the condensed version or the unedited story?" Michael said, attempting to lighten what was getting darker.

"That's up to you, but I would prefer the truth."

Michael pulled away from Dan and moved across the spa. She wanted to look him in the eye. It would be her way of reading his reaction, her way of knowing what to put in and what to leave out.

"Are you sure?" she asked, giving Dan an opportunity to back out of the question.

He nodded and moved to kiss her fully, passionately, on the lips before returning to his former position.

"When I was almost six, my mother, Sean, my brother, and I moved back to Ireland. My parents had divorced. My mother wanted us away from a situation that had gotten bad. That was fine with Sean and me. We loved Ireland because it was where our mother was from, and her family was there.

"When I was seventeen, Sean twenty, our da"—she signed "father" and fingerspelled D-A—"died. It was sudden and unexpected. We returned to Georgia, where I was born, and my da had lived until he died. But it was only Sean and I. Mother stayed in Ireland. Sean and I had traveled before and it had never been a problem. I think my father had shielded us from the feelings of some of his family.

"We were raised Catholic, and in the area of Georgia where my da lived, it didn't make us very popular. Anyway, after the funeral, Sean and some cousins were off, and I was alone in my da's house."

Michael had watched Dan and saw he was taking in the information in a professional manner, nodding with each new bit of information. So far, he seemed to be calm. Michael continued.

"I was waiting for Sean to come home when I heard someone come into the house. I thought it was Sean. It wasn't. There were two of them. I had known them, or of them, all my life, but when I saw them, I knew I was in trouble.

"They tied me to the bed, facedown. I remember one of them telling the other they had cut several stalks of bamboo to teach me a lesson, they were going to whip me." Michael looked away from Dan and fought back the memories of the pain.

"If I remember correctly, each stroke was followed by a Bible quote. In all, I think there were thirty-four quotes."

"Jesus, Michael, I'm so sorry," Dan said.

Michael saw his eyes were filling with tears, but she also saw a question. Did she answer it?

"I suppose they heard Sean return because they rushed out. I remember I had looked at the clock when I thought it was Sean the first time, it was four. When Sean finally came home, it was six. Sean and an older cousin took me to the local doctor, and then we flew home that night."

Dan almost stood up out of the spa. "You didn't go to the police?"

"No."

"Why the hell not?" The rage on his face was almost chilling.

"Because I was in rural Georgia and the family thought I had caused enough trouble."

A string of curses fell from Dan's mouth. Michael let him rant and rave. It would do him good to get it out. Michael had done the same thing when she had returned to Ireland and had been safe in her mother's home.

"Michael." Dan's voice whipped her to attention.

Here it comes, she thought. She didn't wait for the question. She simply signed yes and closed her eyes, not wanting to see his face.

Michael felt herself being gathered into Dan's strong arms. He held her and rocked her back and forth. She felt the tears as they dropped from Dan's handsome face onto her back.

In ragged breaths, Dan repeated. "I'm sorry. Were you raped and nobody was punished?" he asked gently minutes later. He had again moved so he could wrap his arms and legs around her, protecting her.

Michael nodded. What could she say that would change anything?

"Is that why you can't get pregnant?" Dan asked.

"No," Michael said, hoping Dan would drop the subject. He did.

"I think we have stewed long enough, let's get out," Dan said instead.

They toweled each other off and returned naked to bed. Dan wrapped himself around Michael, and together, they drifted off to sleep.

Monday was spent exploring the Rainforest Pyramid at Galveston's Moody Garden, followed by an early dinner at Flying Dutchman restaurant on the Kemah Boardwalk. After they arrived back at the condo, Dan filled the spa up again and filled the bathroom with candles while Michael answered a few messages that had come in from her insurance agent and e-mailed her brother.

Together they spent the remainder of the evening exploring each other's bodies, making love until they were exhausted.

It had been a perfect weekend, Michael thought to herself, as she drifted off to sleep with Dan holding her in his arms.

CHAPTER 21

Catfish had followed him home from church Sunday evening. He hadn't been seen; the young man was between eighteen and twenty, as Catfish followed him into the apartment complex. Waiting until it was after midnight, he approached the young man's door and gently knocked.

The door was opened within a few moments, and Catfish was in. He had tied the man to a chair, securing his hands behind his back, made sure the blinds were all closed, and placed his duffel bag on the kitchen table and unzipped it.

Catfish glanced at his Rolex before removing it from his wrist. It had been twenty minutes since he had rendered the man unconscious. The chloroform should be wearing off any minute. He put on several latex gloves on each hand before pulling out the duct tape. Measuring the length he felt confident would do the job, he careful applied the tape over the man's mouth.

He didn't want the neighbor's woken at one in the morning.

Catfish adjusted the small light he had removed from the duffle bag and focused the light on the face. The boy, because Catfish could see now that he was not quite a man, had no facial hair, just peach fuzz. His hair was dirty brown and tousled from sleep. He had answered the door shirtless and wearing only briefs and a pair of white athletic sox.

Catfish bowed his head and prayed that Jesus would give him the strength to do what he needed to do to this boy. He felt confident as the boy's eyes fluttered open.

Catfish watched interestedly as the pale blue eyes stared sightlessly at him. He could read fear on the kid's face; Catfish understood why anyone would be frightened and cleared his voice.

"I am not going to hurt you. I want you to know that from the start. I want you to do something for me. We are going to spend the day making sure you understand what I need for you to do. If you do as I say, you will be safe. If you don't"—Catfish moved to the boy and reached down and grabbed his crotch—"I will make it very hard for you to fuck your boyfriend again. Do you understand?"

The boy nodded his head quickly.

"Good. Now I know your name is Ron. I know you work at a beauty parlor for your boyfriend, Kev. If you do what I ask, both you and Kev will be okay. If not, I will first kill your little friend, and then I will come after you. Are you ready to learn your lessons?" Catfish asked, enjoying the power he felt over the boy. He might have to teach him a lesson, just for the fun of it, but later, much later.

They worked until six that morning. Catfish took Ron to the bathroom, stripped him, and allowed him to do his business before dragging him by the arms and throwing him on the bed. Using rope, Ron was tied to the bed.

"I'm gonna get a few hours sleep before we continue. I advise you to do the same. If you are good, Ron, I will take that tape off your mouth so you can have something to eat and drink after our nap," Catfish told his captive. Before moving to the other side of the bed to try and sleep, Catfish moved so that he was touching Ron's face with his hand. "If you piss me off, Ron, I will hurt you. Don't piss me off."

At eleven, Catfish woke. He glanced at Ron and found that he hadn't tried anything stupid. He watched the rhythm of Ron's chest move up and down and determined he was asleep.

Catfish ran his eyes over Ron's body. It was young and strong. Catfish was surprised at the rugged condition of this young blind boy's body. It reminded him of some of the girls and boys he had had in Mexico and in Prague over the years. They were young and strong and able to endure the pleasure Catfish liked to have.

With his lovely wife, Eva, his sex life was clean Christian lovemaking. It was never new, never different. He pleased his wife as she pleased him, but he had desired more. It was the one thing about him he blamed on the Abomination, his lust for young bodies. It didn't matter the gender; sex was hot and intense. He took what he wanted, how he wanted it, and didn't have to worry about them.

He couldn't help it; he traced his open hand over Ron's body, waking him. Catfish became excited as he fondled Ron into an erection. It became engorged as Catfish stroked and squeezed. The fear on Ron's face only added to his excitement. As Ron came, so did Catfish.

Within seconds after his climax, Catfish was angry, "You shouldn't have let me do that, Ron. I might have to hurt you now."

The tears rolling from Ron's eyes didn't faze Catfish. He didn't really care. This and the next was just a way of getting to the Abomination.

"Shall we finish this so I can get out of here?"

Catfish spent the rest of Monday repeating the phrase that Ron must be able to repeat on Tuesday. Over and over he said the words. At some point in time, he had removed a small length of bamboo from his bag and, with each word, hit Ron. It wasn't enough to cause any bruises, just enough to drive home the message.

Just before midnight, Catfish sighed and addressed Ron who was red-faced from crying, "I'm going to remove the tape from your mouth and you are going to repeat to me what I have asked you to remember. If you do this without a mistake, I will leave, and you will never have to hear from me again. That is, if you do as you are told to do tomorrow. I will know, remember you can't see me, but I can see you. I will know if you have done what I asked you to do. If you do not, I will come back for you, after I have finished with Kev. If you make any sound other than quietly repeating my words, you will not enjoy the last few seconds of your life. Do you understand?" Catfish asked.

Ron nodded his head slowly.

Catfish took a knife out of his bag and placed the blunt edge on Ron's penis before removing the tape.

"Okay, what are you going to say tomorrow?"

Catfish kept the knife in place as Ron, with ragged breaths, repeated every word that had been drilled into him.

"Where are you supposed to go and who are you supposed to see?"

Again the answers pleased Catfish.

"I have to say, Ron, you have done really well. Remember your life really does depend on doing everything I have asked you and nothing I have warned you against doing. Because you have been such a good boy, I think you deserve a reward."

Catfish removed the knife from Ron's flaccid penis and returned the tape to his lips before Ron could react.

The boy was still tied and was dragged back to the bedroom. Catfish went to the bathroom and stripped out of his clothes in the shower. Checking his pocket, he pulled out several condoms and returned to the bedroom.

Catfish stretched his body over Ron's, whispering in his ear, "I hope you like your reward, I know I will."

After he had exhausted himself, Catfish went to the bathroom to clean himself up. Ron had not disappointed him. Catfish had been sated in every possible way. After he was dressed, he returned to Ron. "Now don't forget," Catfish reminded him before using the chloroform to knock him out again. Once Ron was unconscious, he was untied and the tape removed from his mouth.

Catfish took a few minutes to gather his things, using his mini vacuum to clean up any possible incriminating fibers. He spent a full twenty minutes making sure nothing was left behind. Satisfied he had done his best, he let himself out.

CHAPTER 22

Danton stood at the end of Dan's desk and sipped his coffee, eying Dan. "I have to say, I haven't seen you with that expression on your face . . . Well, I have never seen you with that expression on your face. Michael and you must have had one hell of a weekend." Danton laughed as he slapped Dan's shoulder.

Dan looked up at Danton and saw Garcia heading their way. Since Dan had arrived at the station at seven thirty this morning, he had been getting ribbed unmercifully. Most of the officers had been at O'Brian's last Saturday evening, and each had a comment to make. Dan accepted the harassment as it was intended, good-natured fun. These men and women put their lives on the line as a group and individually every day; they each had a soft spot for the other. If one was doing well, it was cause for celebration.

Dan had left Michael still asleep with a note on the pillow. She had looked so peaceful and relaxed he didn't have the heart to wake her. He would text her later in the day, but for now, he had to concentrate on work.

There had been a murder in the precinct, and the star witness was a deaf woman. She had, unfortunately for her, seen the entire sordid affair. Dan was needed to question her. It was what he did best. Many people who were deaf had a mistrust of the hearing world. Because he had spent almost all his life in the deaf community, Dan could empathize. He had seen his mother and father being taken advantage of, as well as his grandparents on both sides. Dan would be able to help this woman feel at ease and, hopefully, help her feel relaxed enough to tell him what she had seen.

The woman had been considerably traumatized, yet after communicating with her for half an hour, she began to open up. It took the better part of three hours to get her statement. They had looked through mug shots together, and she had picked out the primary suspect.

When they finished, she was feeling better and had promised Dan she would go to her parents' home in Conroe to rest. He had her cell number and her parents' phone number if she needed to be reached.

Dan stopped for lunch before returning to the station. When he arrived, he was met at the front desk by Carson.

"Shit, man, you're popular today," Carson said as he pulled Dan to the side.

"Why's that?" Dan inquired.

"About ten minutes ago, some kid showed up and asked for you. He's really shaken up, but he won't talk to anyone else but you. We put him in interrogation room 3. Captain and Garcia are in there with him."

Dan tried to recall if he had left his card with someone or had a case open in which this kid might be connected with. He couldn't think of one, but that didn't mean anything. Dan started to head toward the back of the station where the interrogation rooms were when Carson stopped him.

"This kid looks like he's been roughed up. I can tell you one thing, poor thing is scared shitless. I think if you were to yell boo, he'd drop." There was no humor in his voice as Carson made the comment.

Dan nodded; it was never easy to see the conditions some of these people came in.

Before Dan could enter the room, Captain Parker stepped out. "Good, it's you. I was about to have Janacek give you a call."

"I just got back from interviewing the witness in the Williams' homicide," Dan said.

"How'd it go?"

"Great. She is gonna be a great witness, and we got a lot of information from her. That guy is as good as convicted."

"It's always nice to catch a case like that once in a while." Parker looked at him for a moment, making Dan uneasy. "Hartman, you remember last week when you went to that hotel on South Telephone Road?"

Dan thought for a minute. "Sure, why?"

"Well, I think this is tied into that case. I got Hernandez to fax over the report with what that Ms. Galvan had been told to tell you. I just got a feeling about this 'cause this kid, name's Ronald Dale, refuses to talk to anyone but you, same as Ms. Galvan."

The chills had begun to work their way up Dan's spine. He had all but forgotten that incident. He had not been able to make sense of it and had figured unless it was something that became relevant, he would forget it. It looked like it might have just become relevant.

"Well, let me see what the kid has to say," Dan said as he pushed past Parker and entered the room.

Ronald Dale was a petite man of eighteen or nineteen years. He was fair-complexioned and had a delicate air about him. His hair was neat, his clothes stylishly put together. The only thing that was out of place was his dark glasses. Dan also noted folded neatly on the table was a cane.

When Dan closed the door behind him, the young man's head snapped up.

"Are you Detective Daniel Hartman?"

The young man's voice was soft yet not effeminate.

"Yes. I understand you wanted to talk to me," Dan said as he pulled a chair out and sat across from Ron.

"I know that Captain Parker and Detective Garcia are in here, who else? It's a woman, I can smell her perfume."

Dan looked around at the small group of officers and Janacek, the stenographer for the station, as their attention focused between the kid and himself.

"That would be Mrs. Janacek. She is here to take down the information you have for us," Dan explained.

"For you, but I have permission for them to stay." Ron's matter-of-fact tone chilled Dan.

"I want to see what you look like. I want to know who it was I . . ." Ron said, letting his voice trail off. Getting up and moving around the table toward Dan, Garcia moved to stop the kid, but Dan waved him off.

Dan allowed Ron to trace his fingers over his face. When Michael had done this, it had been sexual, but Ron's fingers were more analytical in the way they explored. When Ron finished, he returned to his seat.

"Are you the 'Abomination'?" Ron asked.

Dan looked across the table at Ron, then over to Parker. Parker nodded for him to answer the questions. Dan could not figure out how this was tied to him; he would just have to wait and see.

"No, I don't think I am."

"Do you know what . . . who the Abomination is?" There was almost a pleading quality to Ron's voice. He needed to know as much as Dan.

"No, I'm sorry, I don't."

Dan watched as Ron's shoulders sagged for a moment before he continued, "I have a message for you. I have been given answers to some questions that you might ask. If I don't know, I will tell you."

"Go ahead," Parker said.

Dan waited.

Ron took a deep breath and began, "I have warned you, Daniel Hartman. The Abomination is taking over your life. But I also have been told, Jesus has given me the information as to why you were chosen. It is not the Abomination but God himself that has picked you for this holy thing. Together we will rid the earth of this creature. Your life is spared, God has ordained it. But I cannot guarantee that you won't get hurt, I am sure you will. God will help heal any wounds you suffer. Know that I will contact you again, soon. And soon, together, we will kill the Abomination." As Ron finished his practiced speech, he lowered his head into his arms and began to cry.

Everyone in the room was looking at Dan, who was watching Ron. He got up and moved to sit next to the crying man.

"Hartman, do you have any idea what the hell this is about?" Parker asked, taking the chair Dan had vacated.

"No."

"That is fucking weird," Garcia said, making the sign of the cross.

Dan's attention turned back to Ron. He reached over and rubbed the boy's back, comforting him. "Ron, you did a great job. Can you tell us what happened?"

Dan and the other officers listened as Ron told his story. He was holding something back. Dan was certain of it but didn't pressure the boy, not just yet.

"Can you tell us anything you can remember about the man himself?"

Ron had pulled himself together. "Yeah, his accent was really thick, Deep South, maybe. I was tied up the entire time, so I never got a chance to figure out what he looked like."

"Can we go and search your apartment, see if we can find anything we can use to catch this SOB?"

"Sure, but he told me to tell you, you wouldn't find anything. I believe him, you know."

Dan watched as Ron folded his hands in his lap and waited.

"Give us the address, and we will get someone over to your apartment right now," Parker addressed Ron. When Ron had given him the information, Parker and Garcia left the room. Janacek followed, leaving Dan alone with Ron.

"What did he do to you?" Dan asked.

"I told you," Ron said a bit too defensively.

"I know what you said, but it's just me and you now. I know he did something else, I can tell. I haven't been a cop this long not to read the signs. He hurt you in some way. I can help if you let me," Dan waited.

"Are you sure it's just you and me?" Ron asked, moving his head around as if scanning the room for other people.

"Yes."

"He told me to tell you if we are alone. You can't tell anyone else, or he said he would come back for me. You have to promise!" Ron was almost frantic with his request.

"I will do everything I can to help and to keep my promise." Dan chose his words carefully making sure he could use this information if needed.

Ron told Dan the rest of the story he had left out when the others were present in the room. Dan felt sick. The bastard was twisted. Ron remembered not only what had been done to him but also the words that were used.

This information along with the entire "Abomination," God, Jesus thing gave Dan the feeling they were dealing with one sick and twisted asshole. The problem was Dan had no idea what the hell the bastard was talking about. He had looked the word "Abomination" up in the dictionary, yet that had left him more confused, still not answering the hundreds of questions rolling around in his head.

"Ron, I want to thank you for coming in. Do you have a place to go and feel safe?" Dan inquired.

Ron had a friend, Kev, whom he could stay with. But the man knew about Kev and had threatened to hurt him if he hadn't done exactly what he was told.

Just as Dan was going to ask another question, Ron's cell phone rang.

"Answer it."

"Hello." Ron's voice was tentative.

Dan watched as the color drained from his face and the phone slipped from his fingers. He scooped up the phone and placed it to his ear but heard nothing but a dial tone.

"What did he say?" Dan snapped, trying to get Ron to focus.

In a shaky voice, Ron answered, "He said I had done well and that Kev and I were blessed as queers could be and safe." Ron broke down into tears.

CHAPTER 23

"What the Sam Hill is all this shit about?" Parker yelled across his desk as Dan walked into his office, a half hour later.

Dan looked at Garcia, who was standing by the door. Garcia raised an eyebrow at Dan. "I honestly don't know. I have no idea who either Ms. Galvan is or who Ronald Dale is. I haven't any idea what the hell the bastard means by Abomination. Shit, I had to look up the word in the dictionary just to have a general idea. I have no idea why I have been singled out by this psycho, but I can tell you one thing. After you left, that poor kid told me what that sick son of a bitch did to him."

Dan spent the next few minutes filling in the details. Both Parker and Garcia looked pissed. "Whoever this man is, he's one sick mother fucker! I don't know who he's fixed on. I really don't think it's me, but I could be wrong."

Dan got up and moved to the window. He looked out wondering if he was being watched even now. "He called when we were still in interrogation, told Ron he had done a good job. Ron agreed to a search and didn't have any sort of transmitting device on him, so how the hell did he know Ron was finished with his part of this sick game?"

"Maybe someone was in the station house who was watching the proceeding," Garcia commented.

Parker shook his head. "No, the interrogation room can't be seen from the front of the station. If someone was watching, they would have had to have been in the squad room. Have Carson check the surveillance camera to see who was in the room at the time Dale was in there with us. I am going to turn the transcript of this interview and Hernandez's notes over to our profiler and see what he can come up with. In the meantime, Hartman, I want you to report anything out of the ordinary. I want you to tap your phone, just in case he calls you. He seems to want to do this in public, but who knows?"

Dan agreed, as well as to a few other precautions. He didn't want to put himself or, for that matter, Michael or David and his family in danger. If this nutjob was going after strangers, maybe he would go after someone closer to Dan. Parker had agreed to put a discreet tail on David and Kelly as well as Michael. Together the men decided it would be better not to say anything and just wait and see.

Dan was exhausted, and it was only four.

CHAPTER 24

Michael had paid her insurance agent a visit. The money for the reimbursement of her house and its contents had been wired to Michael's accounts. After signing the stack of papers the agent had for her and following the instructions her brother had given her this morning, she found herself in downtown Houston at La Branch Street, between Texas and Crawford.

She pulled into the parking garage of the old hotel being converted into lofts and headed into the sales office. She was met at the door by Amy Andrews.

"Ms. Braun, I am so glad you could make it. Mr. Fitzpatrick called and told us to expect you. He wanted you to see unit 8B. That is on the penthouse floor. There are only four units on the eighth floor. It's a town house, so really, it is a quarter of the eighth and ninth floor. Are you ready to see it?"

Michael followed the perky blonde into the private elevator that serviced the eighth-floor penthouses. She was amazed that Amy could walk in such a tight skirt and high heels. She had worn her share of tight skirts and high heels, but Amy was teetering on dangerous.

Michael watched as Amy slid a key card into an electronic receptacle. Amy turned to explain, "The private elevator is located in the center of a large rectangular foyer. As you can see the elevator has a door on either side of the car." Amy indicated to the sophisticatedly paneled doors. "We have already decorated the foyer in an understated elegance. Each penthouse has a set of double doors, solid metal inlayed with rich woods, which open up into the two-story foyer of the penthouse apartments." A gentle bell sounded as the elevator doors silently opened. Michael watched as Amy walked to 8B and threw open the doors with a flourish. "Here we are!" Amy announced.

The apartment was beautiful with its open floor plan and vast expanse of windows. The penthouse foyer was polished marble, which led into the first-floor living room. It was so large, Michael was certain she could have fit her old house just in the foyer and living room alone.

"The first floor has the master suite, the living room, a gourmet chef's kitchen, and two and a half baths. The second floor has three bedrooms, two en suites, an office, an exercise room, and an additional bathroom. So all together there are four bedrooms, five and a half baths, which cover 5,600 square feet. Mr. Fitzpatrick instructed me to accept your payment of $100,000. Of course, you know that the apartment sells for $2.6 million."

Michael almost choked when Amy told her the cost of the apartment, but it had all been worked out. Amy would get her hefty commission; Michael, a ridiculous place to live that was safe and secure. Sean would get a tax write-off.

Michael took her checkbook out of her purse and wrote a check for the amount agreed upon. Her hand was shaking as she signed her name. Amy's hand was shaking as she accepted the check with a giggle. "This is my first commission on these properties," she confessed, glancing side to side as if checking to make sure they were alone.

Did well! Michael thought to herself.

"Oh, Ms. Braun, Mr. Fitzpatrick told me to tell you that the decorator would be here tomorrow, and you are to meet with him or her, I don't remember, at eleven, if you can, of course. If not, he asked me to ask you to let him know."

Michael nodded as she withdrew a notepad and pen out of her purse. She wrote a thank-you note to Amy, who told her she was happy to help and she would have the contacts and keys ready tomorrow for Michael to pick up.

After leaving the loft, Michael headed to Katy and David and Kelly's house. She had texted Kelly earlier in the day to see if she could come over for visit. Kelly had said it would be great, and they spent several hours chasing three-year-olds and catching up.

"So was I right?" Kelly asked Michael after the kids had been put down for the afternoon nap.

"About what?" Michael hoped her face was reflecting the innocent mask she was trying to put forth.

"Oh, don't play dumb with me, sister. Is he the most incredible lover you have ever had or what, and don't keep any sleazy details to yourself," Kelly said as he moved from the chair to sit on the sofa next to Michael.

She began to cry, something she had done when she discussed Dan with her brother.

"Oh, honey," Kelly said as he took her hands. "You have it bad, don't you?"

Michael looked through the tears at Kelly. She had had relationships before, even thought she was in love, but this was something new, different, and terrifying. She told Kelly so.

"He scares me, Kelly," Michael confessed. "When he looks at me, I don't know what he is seeing, but if it's me, it's a 'me' I didn't know was there. He is incredible but tender and loving, gentle, and giving. I can't believe he's been there all this time, and I didn't know it."

"Well, things happen the way they're supposed to happen. I really believe that, Michael, so you weren't meant to meet until this time. There is always a reason. It was the same with David and me. I knew about him, you talked about him all the time, but I just never met him until you introduced us. Now, I guess, we are repaying the favor." Kelly looked at his watch and stood up.

"You have to get out of here, or you'll never get home. You know how traffic is on I-10?"

Michael was escorted to her car, making Kelly promise to kiss the kids and David for her. Just before getting in the car, she stopped and waved at Kelly. "Sean is going to be here this weekend. He is coming over to the condo on Friday night for a barbecue. You guys come, you know, Sean really liked you guys, and the triplets love him. Be there at seven, call David as soon as you get in the house, will you?"

After securing a promise from Kelly, Michael drove home or what she was beginning to think as home.

It took almost an hour and a half to reach the condo on Stanford. The house was quiet and dark. Michael went around opening blinds and turning on the stereo before texting Dan.

"How has your day been?" Michael texted.

"You don't want to know" flashed across the LCD display of her iPhone.

"That bad?"

"Worse."

"Sorry. When do you think you will get home?"

"I'm leaving at six and coming straight home to you."

Michael smiled when she read those words. "Well . . .," Michael typed, "I'll be here waiting." She laughed silently to herself as her imagination began thinking of ways to help improve Dan's day.

"Thank God. Love you."

Michael didn't respond. She would show him how she felt about him when he got home.

When Michael had talked to Sean Monday, using the video relay on the computer in the study, she had told him of her feelings and of her impression of Dan. Sean was concerned that the relationship was moving too fast. Michael agreed that maybe it was, but it was too late to stop it now.

It was at that time Sean told Michael about the building he had bought in downtown Houston and his idea for her to buy into ownership of the penthouse with the money she would be getting for her destroyed home.

"I am not in Houston that much, but when I am, I would have a place to stay. The fans couldn't bother me. I just signed that new contract with Seattle and needed some investments. I had known about the old hotel being converted, so three months ago, I closed the deal. I didn't want to say anything to you, but after what happened, I want you to move there. The security is top-notch."

Michael listened and agreed that it was a good idea. If for some reason she needed a place, she would have one. Sean told her he would pay for the furnishings and decor. He asked Michael to decorate the penthouse to her tastes, and he would pay her a monthly salary for keeping up the penthouse and keeping an eye on the management of the building.

"When are you going back to work?" Sean asked after finishing up with the details of what he needed from Michael regarding the building and the penthouse.

"After the first of the year. I need some time, you know. David and I worked it out."

She watched the plasma monitor of the computer carefully as a worried look crossed over her brother's face. "Do you have any ideas?" he finally asked the question she was expecting.

"No."

"Could it be, you know," he asked, not seeming to be able to say the name.

"I don't know how. He doesn't know where I am, and you and I are always discreet when we meet. I just don't know."

They ended their conversation expressing their happiness at being able to see each other soon. Michael would wait to tell Dan about the penthouse this weekend; maybe she would let Sean tell him. She knew that was the chicken's way out, but she didn't care.

The clock in the living room struck the half hour, spurring Michael into action. By the time Michael heard the garage door open, she was ready. She moved to where Dan would see her as soon as he rounded the corner from the garage. She had never done this sort of thing before and hoped it would work.

CHAPTER 25

Dan was exhausted. It had been a hell of a day, to say the least. After they had written up the report on the Abomination Man, as he was being called at the station, Dan had to sit through an interview with the department profiler, hoping they could determine exactly what this individual had in mind. So far they were clueless. Aside from Dan, to whom no one could figure out that connection, there really wasn't much to go on.

The garage door closed behind him as he got out of the car. All he wanted was to get out of this monkey suit, put up his feet, have a nice dinner and a beer, and spend some quite time with Michael.

The lights in the kitchen were off, but light came from the direction of the living room. Dan rounded the corner and stopped dead in his tracks.

Michael stood in high heels, red thong and bra, and nothing else, except a beer in her hand.

She smiled wickedly at him, and his knees went weak as other parts of his body came to attention.

"How was your day, dear?" she signed one handed.

He didn't answer her but went to her. He took the beer from her hand and set it on the end table. She started to remove his shirt. He stopped her with a kiss. It was deep and long. Dan's tongue tasted her mouth. She was sweet and heady, better than any beer. Dan wanted to drink her up.

As he continued to kiss Michael, he worked his way out of his shoes, his jacket, and with some assistance from Michael's slender hands, his pants.

Dan lost his balance, and together, they fell to the living room floor. "Are you all right?" he asked. She ran her hand down his chest and inside his briefs as a response.

"I needed you," Dan whispered as their kiss became frenzied.

Dan touched her hardened nipple through the lacy material that covered only the bottom half of Michael's breasts. He moved from her mouth, down her neck, to capture the tip of her breast with his lips.

Michael's hand was working her way along his erection, bringing him nearer to climax than he was ready for. "No," he told her and moved to capture her arms over her head. "No," Dan repeated as his attention returned to her mouth.

Dan had lost control. In the back of his mind, he could hear himself say to slow down, be gentle, but he didn't heed the warning. With one hand cuffing her wrists, Dan used the other to remove her bra, and with a quick jerk, the thin material of her panties was torn off her.

Dan looked into Michael's face; her lips were parted, her eyes staring into his. He watched as she mouthed "I love you." It sent him over the edge. He reached between her legs and stroked and explored with his fingers. Everything he did had an edge of desperation.

When Michael's hips started to match his movement, Dan pulled her up to her feet turned her so she faced away from him. He kissed the ridges on her back and moved his hands to cup her breasts. Michael's head fell back and rested against his chest. The sharp spines of her hair were erotic against his hot skin.

"Michael," he gasped as he bent her over the back of the couch and entered her from behind. He plunged deep into her with each hard stroke.

Dan didn't hear, didn't see, only felt. As he came, Michael threw her head back, and Dan could feel her body vibrate with her own release.

It took several minutes for Dan to come out of the sexual fog, but when he did, he was horrified. He had all but attacked and raped Michael.

"Oh, shit, Michael, I am so sorry," he said as he pulled himself out of her and pulled her around.

The expression on her face was not what he had expected. Her kiss-swollen lips were twisted in a grin that was not particularly ladylike. She touched his face with one hand as she rested the other on his chest.

He waited; he knew he had probably ended the relationship. He had never been so . . . so . . . crazed in all his life. He was working on his excuses in the silence.

"Wow!" Michael started. "That was more than I expected, but I am glad it worked."

Dan looked at her again, seeing the humor on her face.

"I didn't mean to take you right here. I can't believe I did that."

"Why not? It was my intention to help you forget the shitty day you had. Did it work?" Michael stepped into him and kissed his chin.

"I'll say. You're not hurt or angry?" Dan just had to ask. "Wait," he interrupted himself. "Did you say before I attacked you like a horny teenager, did you say—"

"I love you," Michael supplied the words he was looking for.

Dan took her in his arms and lifted her, carrying her to the bedroom. After he placed her on the bed, he moved himself on top of her. He wanted to feel her; she was like a place he could lose himself in.

"Michael, where did you come from?" he asked, kissing her, this time with as much gentleness and tenderness as he could.

"I think the same things, but you know what Kelly told me? He said, 'Things happen when they're supposed to happen.' We weren't ready to meet until we did. I believe him."

Dan sat up bracing his weight with his bent knees. He looked down at Michael. She looked back. The trust and love, yes, love, he saw in her beautiful violet eyes humbled him. He wasn't sure what he had done to deserve this woman. The one thing he knew for certain, more than anything he had ever known before in his life, was he didn't want to ever be without her.

"Michael, I want you to live here," he said, watching to see how his words affected her.

"Dan, I am living here." Her expression hadn't changed.

"No, I mean"—he placed his hand over his heart, then over hers—"I don't want you to leave, ever."

The change was subtle, but Dan saw it. Michael reached up and covered his mouth with her hand. He kissed her palm.

"I am here for as long as you want me," she told him.

Dan saw the words, but something else was being said. He didn't know what she meant. Her signs had said one thing. Her expression backed up the signs, but there was more. Dan was terrified to ask.

He rolled off her and pulled her so her head rested on his chest. This position allowed for him to see her sign yet hold her at the same time.

"There will never be a time I don't want you." Dan's voice was strong and adamant.

Michael simply pulled his arms tighter around her.

CHAPTER 26

When Michael finally opened her eyes after lying for what seemed like hours, it was still dark, and the clock's red digits declared 5:52 a.m.

She and Dan had stayed in bed for the balance of the evening. Dan was tired and had only gotten out of bed to clean up and get something to drink. Michael hadn't been hungry, and it seemed, neither had Dan.

This morning, however, she was starved. Dan's clock would be going off about six thirty, and Michael decided that she would get up and cook a nice breakfast. Carefully, she slipped out of bed and headed upstairs to the third floor to wash her face and brush her teeth. The house was cold, and she needed her robe and some socks for her feet.

The coffee was already brewing when she descended into the kitchen. She pulled bacon, eggs, and butter out of the refrigerator. The range had a built-in griddle so Michael set out enough bacon for the two of them and adjusted the flame.

She was finishing with the turkey bacon and already scrambling the eggs in a bowl when she heard Dan moving around upstairs. She poured herself and Dan each a mug of coffee. Michael was about to go up and deliver his coffee, but Dan came down instead. He was wearing his Mickey Mouse T-shirt and boxer briefs as he moved around the island and kissed Michael good morning.

She handed him his coffee and kissed him back.

"I thought you might be hungry this morning," she said as she put four pieces of bread into the toaster.

"You'd be right. Having you around makes me hungry for all sorts of things," Dan replied as he pinched her bottom through her robe.

"Do you want me to wait until you shower, or do you want to eat first?" Michael asked with her finger poised on the latch for the toaster.

"Let's have breakfast first." Dan sat at the bar and watched her as she finished cooking.

"I like this," Dan said after a few minutes.

"What?" Michael inquired as she finished cooking the eggs.

"Having you here like this." Dan moved off the stool and poured himself a fresh cup of coffee, topping off Michael's as well.

Michael looked over at him. She liked it too. "What's not to like," she told herself.

"Sit," Michael ordered as she put the plates on the bar and moved around to join Dan.

"So what's your day like today?" Dan asked.

Michael hadn't told him about the penthouse yet and wasn't really sure how to do that after last night. She had asked Kelly to meet her at the building at eleven to help her figure out what to do with the decor if he could find a sitter. After that, she wasn't sure.

"My brother asked me to see to some business for him. He has a few irons in the fire in Houston. I am his official gofer here."

"I know you have a brother, but I don't know who he is," Dan said before stuffing a forkful of eggs into his mouth.

"Well, that is going to be taken care of Friday night. Brother Sean is going to be here for the weekend. He is coming over for dinner Friday along with David, Kelly, and the kids. They all know each other. I wanted to ask you if it would be okay if Sean stayed here. He could stay at a hotel. God knows he can afford it, but I like to have him near when he is here. If he stays in a hotel, it's hard for us to spend time together because the damn paparazzi hound him." Michael looked over her mug and smiled sweetly at Dan.

"You know I don't mind, but now I really am curious about your brother." Dan took Michael's hand.

She winked at him. "Well, Friday will be a surprise for you then, I'm not saying anything."

When Dan had finished his breakfast, he stood up and moved behind Michael. "I have ways of making you talk," he teased her.

"I'm sure you do, but I have a high threshold. It could take hours and hours of that particular type of torture you have in mind before I might talk," Michael said, swiveling on her stool so she was face-to-face with Dan. "And besides, you are out of time this morning. You can try tonight if you want, but I can't guarantee you'll learn anything. I can guarantee though, I'll enjoy myself."

Dan kissed her. "You are bad," he scolded her.

"I know," she agreed and sent him up to shower and ready himself for work.

She cleaned the kitchen and went to the third floor to get ready for her day. While she was in the shower, Dan came in and kissed her good-bye. He told her to text if she needed anything or if she just wanted to say hello.

He also made her promise she would be careful and keep her doors locked. She promised she would and sent him on his way.

Michael met Kelly downtown at ten thirty and, with his help, went over the paperwork that needed to be signed on the penthouse with the title company. Only half the paperwork was relevant for her, but Michael paid attention while the man discussed closing costs, fees, and amendments.

At eleven, Doris Hanson, a decorator from the deaf community and quite respected in the hearing world, showed up, and the three of them took the elevator to the eighth floor.

"Holy shit" was Kelly's comment when the elevator opened up and they stepped into the grand foyer then through the double doors of the penthouse, Kelly signed the equivalent so that Doris Hanson was included in the conversation.

"It is a great space," Doris added, explaining she had already previewed the penthouse and had worked up several potential themes for the decor.

"I'm going to go and check this place out while you two start figuring out where the couches are going to go." Kelly laughed at himself as he disappeared down the hall.

Michael and Doris went from room to room discussing ideas for furnishings, area rugs, and wall coverings. Michael had decided on a simple arts-and-crafts motif for the entire penthouse. The warm colors and simplicity of style, with its earth tones and natural color palette, made Michael feel safe and comfortable. Doris, for her part, was pleased with the choices and went on to discuss material options for seating, wood types for tables, armoires, and cabinets, as well as types of floor covering for each room.

Kelly popped in from time to time to make helpful or sarcastic comments and inform Michael of each new impossible cool discovery he made.

It took Michael and Doris about two hours to go from room to room and discuss what was needed. Sean had given Doris a budget for doing the entire penthouse, so all that was expected of Michael was to make the choices of what was to go in what space. She and Sean had similar tastes, so she was confident he would approve.

When Doris had left, Kelly descended upon her, "You have got to see this." He grabbed her hand and pulled her through the penthouse to the kitchen. Behind a door Michael had thought was a pantry was a small room with a door to the left and a staircase to the right. "That door"—Kelly pointed to the door to the left—"is the emergency exit from this floor. It hooks up with the stairs on the seventh floor. The fire door is made so you can get out, but no one can get into your private space. Although there is a main emergency exit that does go to the roof, it just doesn't go through this way."

He pulled her to the right and ascended the stairs. At the top of the landing, Kelly opened the door to the roof. On the roof was a hot tub, a top-of-the-line grill built into a counter, a small refrigerator, a tap for a keg, and other features to guarantee the best outdoor party available in the outdoor kitchen.

Half of the space was covered with a pergola while the rest was exposed to the sun.

"This is fantastic," Michael said as she turned to survey the space. The view wasn't the best since the downtown Houston skyscrapers towered over her, but the space itself was built to enjoy, and it became her favorite part of the penthouse.

"I really hate you," Kelly said as he kissed her cheek, "and I expect to be entertained extravagantly often."

Michael looked at Kelly, motioning him back to the door. As they returned to the kitchen, Michael said, "I haven't told Dan about this. I think I'm going to let Sean explain this to him, man-to-man. But at least"—Michael stopped and faced Kelly—"I have a place to go if . . ."

"I don't want to hear that shit. Let's go have lunch, I'm starved." Kelly stopped her from saying she would have a place to go if and when Dan tired of her.

Despite her demeanor, Michael just wasn't that confident that anyone would or could love her. That was why Dan both terrified her and amazed her.

They ate downtown at the Kobe Sushi Bar, Michael having a couple of beers with her meal. Kelly promised they would be at Dan's on Friday night before leaving for the suburbs.

Michael drove herself to Katy and the station where Dan worked and decided to see how he would react if she just stopped by. She wasn't testing him, not really. However, if she was going to be in his life, she needed to know what boundaries he would set. Many of the nurses in David's office had said their boyfriends or husbands didn't like for them to just show up at their place of business.

She was dressed for the cool weather of mid-November in wool pants and matching accented sweater. Her shoes were comfortable flats. Her makeup was minimal. There was nothing Michael could do to her hair, and she tried not to worry about it.

She found a parking spot quickly but, before getting out of her car, reapplied her lipstick and wrote on her ever-present notepad, "I would like to see Detective Hartman. Ms. Braun."

She found her way to the front desk and handed the note to the officer stationed there. He looked her over and punched a number on the switchboards.

"Hartman," he spoke into the phone, keeping his eye on Michael, "there is a Ms. Braun here to see you."

Michael was instructed to have a seat by the officer. *Maybe this is a bad idea,* she thought. *He's busy and I should have just called.*

The doors that led into the interior of the station flew open, and Dan, flushed in the face, moved quickly toward Michael, who stood up.

"What's wrong?" Dan held her at arm's length, a worried expression on his face.

"Shit," Michael signed when she realized that her unannounced visit had caused Dan to believe something had happened. "No, nothing, I'm fine. I was just on my way to the condo from seeing Kelly and I thought I would stop."

She watched as Dan sank into a chair. He reached for her hand and gently pulled her down to sit next to him. In ASL, he said, "I was terrified something happened." She watched as he closed his eyes and took a deep breath.

"I didn't mean to worry you. I just thought it would be nice to stop by and say hello, I won't do it again." Michael felt guilty and stupid. It had been a bad idea.

"No, I'm glad you're here." He leaned over and kissed her. "Come on and see where I work."

Michael hesitantly followed Dan through the doors and into the station. She recognized several of the officers who had been at the pub the week before. Garcia crossed the room to say hello, slapping Dan on the back as he passed him.

"Hello, Ms. Braun, you look lovely today," Garcia said as he took her hand and gallantly kissed her knuckles.

"You're a gentleman. Thank you," Michael signed and waited for Dan to translate, which he did. Then added on his own, "But she goes home with me."

Garcia laughed and walked off. Michael was led though a maze of desks before coming to Dan's. She looked over the disorderly top, pausing at the family photo of David, Kelly, and the triplets.

Michael raised an eyebrow at the photo and asked, "You catch flack for that?"

Dan seemed confused for a moment, then following the line of her gaze, smiled. "Only once. Some asshole said something. I heard about it after the fact, but Carson, someone told me later, threw a fit. Heard he reamed the guy out but good."

That impressed Michael. Dan was lucky enough to work with a bunch of really nice people; not everybody did. Dan offered her his chair and sat on the edge of his desk.

He asked her how her day had been, and she told him she had spent the morning taking care of business for her brother. She also let him know that Kelly had tagged along, they had had sushi for lunch, and after her stop here, she was heading home. She corrected herself and said "to your house."

Dan moved closer to her, changing from sign to using his voice, "No, you had it right the first time. Home." He kissed her lightly on the cheek.

A throat was cleared behind her, and Dan straightened up. "Captain Parker, I would like to introduce you to Michael Braun, my girlfriend."

Michael stood up and faced the captain. He was a tall man in his late fifties, with a full head of white hair and a distinguished face. She accepted his offered hand and liked that he shook her hand as an equal.

"So you are the mystery woman I have heard so much about," he said, releasing her hand.

Michael looked at Dan and said, "It's nice to meet you."

"I haven't said anything." Dan looked at her, raising his arms up in surrender.

"No, ma'am, not Hartman here. He's pretty tight-lipped, but I have to say you made one hell of an impression on half of the squad here last weekend," Parker said, his eye twinkling mischievously.

Michael laughed and looked up at the captain. "I do what I can."

Parker smiled and, with a nod, left.

"I'd better go," Michael said.

"Yeah, if you don't leave, I'll never finish this paperwork I'm working on. And if I don't finish, I don't go home." Dan took her hand, and together, they headed back toward the front.

They had almost reached the doors to the lobby when someone called to Dan, "Hey, don't forget you have a meeting with the profiler."

Another voice yelled back, "Yeah, don't be an Abomination!"

The word froze Michael in midstep. Her knees buckled and she went down. Dan caught her before she hit the floor. "Jesus, Michael, are you okay?" His panicked voice rang in her ears.

She looked up at him, seeing him and several other men as they helped her to a chair. That was what the man had been screaming as he attacked her, "Abomination, you are an Abomination, Jesus has sent me to remove you." He had said it over and over with each punch, every slap. She knew that voice; she would always know that voice.

"Michael?" Dan's voice was near her face. "Honey, are you all right?"

Michael squared her shoulders and smiled up at Dan. She waved her hand as if bushing back the dust in the air. "I just slipped. The soles of the shoes aren't very good." She lied. It didn't matter; she needed to get out of here and away from Dan, just for a while so she could decide what to do. Did she call Detective Boudreaux or tell Dan and let Dan take care of it? Shit, this was her responsibility. Why did all of a sudden she feel as if she could turn her life over to a man she had only known for less than a month.

"I'm embarrassed," she said as she got up and thanked the men who had moved to help.

Dan didn't say anything but kept his arm around her waist as he walked her to her car.

"Michael, are you really all right?" Dan asked as he pulled her to him.

Michael wanted to scream that she wasn't all right, that she was terrified because she knew who had attacked her. But she felt certain he had already left Houston and wouldn't be back. He couldn't take the chance of attacking her again, could he?

Michael kissed him. Not a "good-bye see you later" sort of kiss; it was a desperate attempt to cling to something that was good.

"I'm going home. See you later, okay?" she said as she unlocked her car.

"Michael, I want you to text me when you get home, please," Dan urged before letting her go.

Michael promised.

CHAPTER 27

Somehow she arrived home. Her mind was spinning a thousand miles an hour. Why hadn't she remembered that voice, those words? It was the same voice from when she was seventeen. They were the same words she had heard at five. Michael was sure she knew who had attacked her. She had been so careful. Both she and Sean had, for the past twelve years, been careful not to be seen together in public. It had been for his protection as much as for hers.

Michael went straight to the computer when she arrived back at the condo. After using her iPhone to call Sean's assistant to get him to his computer, Michael waited until his body appeared on the plasma monitor and his deeply accented voice filled the speakers.

Michael tried but failed not to go into a full panic. "Sean, it's him." Tears were rolling down her face. "It's him. What am I going to do?"

She couldn't breathe. It was as if a hand had reached in and was squeezing the air out of her lungs.

Michael heard Sean yell, "Michael, calm down!" His voice was a distant echo.

She stood up and moved around the room. "I can't, Sean. I'm scared." Her body was wracked by violent shaking. "I can't."

Michael collapsed to the floor. She screamed, with only the sound of air escaping from her lungs to fill the room. She could hear Sean calling her name, trying to help her find some focus. Finally, he told her he was there when she was ready.

She didn't know how long the panic had gripped her, but she looked up, and Sean's tearstained face looked back at her.

"I'll be there tomorrow," he told her.

Michael drew a deep breath. "I don't think he is here. I think he would have contacted me by now. You know how he likes to scare me, he gets a thrill out of it." She wiped her face and blew her nose.

"How did he find you?" Sean asked the question she had repeatedly asked herself since she had left the police station.

"I don't know. We're so careful," she said. "Sean, maybe you shouldn't come. You just signed that big contract with Seattle, and I saw you're in negotiations with Nike. It might not be smart."

"Fuck you, Michael. Do you think that any of that is more important than you?" Sean's angry voice shook the speakers. "The bastard has controlled our life almost since we were born. I'm tired of it, and it's gonna stop now."

Michael was shaking her head. "You worked too hard to lose everything because of me," she warned.

"Do you think people give a shit about that? Really, Michael, you've let him control your entire life, almost thirty years. You have allowed him to keep you, keep us in this little cage of fear! I don't understand why we have let him do this."

"You know why." Michael glared at him.

Sean ignored her. "You have met this wonderful man. If he is anything like his brother, I think for the first time you are really in love. Are you ready to give that up without a fight?" Sean's words carried a dangerous edge to them. It had been a long time since she had heard it.

"But—"

"No more, Michael. I'll be there tomorrow instead of Friday. We'll figure this out. In the meantime, pull yourself together and get on with it. If he's there, you would have known by now. Just listen to your copper boyfriend and keep your eyes open." Sean didn't disconnect; he waited for her to respond.

"Sean"—Michael returned to the chair in front of the computer—"I know you're right, but he really hurt me."

"I know."

"I don't want to lose Dan."

"I know."

"It's just that I've never felt this way."

"I know, honey, I know."

Michael looked at her brother. He was tall and handsome, thirty-two, and single. Maybe it was time to let go and not live in the fear that seemed to have been part of their lives since they were born. Sean deserved to have a life and not have to worry all the time about her. She smiled at him.

"I love you." Michael didn't sign the simple hand sign that was associated with that saying but signed each word, slowly, so he could see.

"I love you back. Really, Michael, you need to pull yourself together before Dan gets home and sees your face all puffy and swollen. Ya look like crap!" His tone was playful, teasing. It was just what she needed to pull herself up by her bootstraps and get it together.

"Thanks."

"Hey, what are older brothers for?" He blew her a kiss before adding, "I'll get a driver at the airport to bring me to the penthouse. Meet me there at three, and we can smuggle me back to your place."

"Okay, see you tomorrow."

Michael took a shower and changed clothes. Sean was right; if her attacker was still around, she would have known. Anytime in the past, before she had finished college, changed her name, and moved to Texas, he hounded her, letting Michael know he was watching her. It was part of his game. Find her, harass her, and if possible, which she hadn't allowed to happen since she was seventeen, hurt her.

But it had really been for Sean that she insisted they keep their relationship a secret. He had been safe all these years, but Michael wasn't sure if that was still the case. She assumed it was. Sean had been on TV, in print, even had a feature article in *Sports Illustrated.* So it wasn't as if he couldn't have been found. She had always been the target. By not being seen in Sean's life, she protected herself as well as him.

As far as Dan was concerned, she was worried for nothing, maybe. She would have to talk to him about her past, her family, but not yet, not just yet. For now she was going to bask in his love for her. It might not last, but she was going to make it last as long as she could.

She prepared dinner and had the dining-room table set with wine and candles when Dan came home. Unlike the evening before, Michael greeted him with a kiss and wrapped her arms around him, refusing to let go.

"What's wrong?" Dan asked, gently pulling Michael back.

"I just missed you today," she said in a half-truth.

"I missed you too, but I saw you not that long ago," Dan responded as he ran his hands down her back.

She shrugged her shoulders and asked, "Are you hungry?"

Dan went upstairs to change while Michael put the food on the table and poured the wine. She took a seat and waited for him to return.

CHAPTER 28

Dan changed out of his suit and redressed in jeans and a sweatshirt. Michael was quieter than normal, having a "deer in the headlights" look in her violet eyes. Something had spooked her, he knew that. He was sure it had been something she had seen or heard at thc station but couldn't place it. He had spent the balance of the day despite the conversations with the profiler and other tasks he had completed, trying to figure out what it had been.

Maybe if he let her be, she would tell him. He hoped she would, but he also knew people who had suffered a violent attack suffered from post-traumatic syndrome and went through bad spells. Perhaps he could get her to see someone; David could help him with this or maybe Michacl's brother when he came.

Whatever she needed he would do for her.

They enjoyed dinner, keeping the conversation light. Dan helped clean the kitchen, and together, they finished a bottle of wine. Dan suggested they watch some TV, enjoy a fire in the fireplace, and just relax. Michael agreed.

Before the ten o'clock news, they had gone to bed. Dan had turned the stereo onto the jazz station and adjusted the volume so the melodies were just a part of the ambient noise of the room. Dan stripped naked and crawled into bed next to Michael, whose warm body relaxed as she curled up around Dan.

He kissed her forehead and simply held her. He was nearly asleep when he felt the pressure of her lips on his. Dan opened his eye. "Make love to me," she whispered with her hands.

He did.

His lovemaking was slow and easy, unlike the night before. Together they touched, stroked, tasted, and gazed upon each other. It was truly making love. Dan shared his soul with Michael; Michael shared hers in return.

When they came, it was with an intense passion that shocked Dan to his core. He had never thought this slow, taking-of-your-time way would have been so incredible.

They kissed and still pleased each other longer into the night until, exhausted, Michael fell asleep.

For the longest time after, Dan watched Michael sleep. He took her in, the way the blanket had slipped to expose the top of her breast, how her leg worked its way from under the covers then back again. Michael's slender hand reached for him even in her sleep. He placed his hand in hers.

The swelling and bruising had long since vanished. The fairness of her skin contrasted with his dark olive complexion. Michael fit him in every way possible a woman fit a man.

His breath caught, he watched her as if with a blink of an eye she would disappear like smoke. Dan closed his eyes, still picturing her lying there. Slowly, as if afraid, he opened his eyes. She was still there.

It was then he realized that very second when he opened his eyes, he would never let her go.

Oh, shit. he thought silently. Dan had never been here. He had been engaged before, but it had been an evolution of a relationship that had happened for the wrong reasons. Maybe he would call David or, better yet, just talk to him when he was here Friday. David and Kelly had been in a stable relationship for almost eleven years. They shared the triplets, David being the biological father. Kelly's sister had carried the triplets, having agreed to the in vitro fertilization and surrogate motherhood. If anyone could tell him what to do next, it would be his "older" brother.

Dan lay down. He had found the woman he was going to spend the rest of his life with; now all he had to do was figure out how to ask this incredible woman to marry him.

CHAPTER 29

At two thirty the next day, Michael was pulling up to the La Branch Street Lofts. She had opted to park in the parking garage of the building. This would allow Sean to pour his six-foot-eleven-inch frame into her Audi A5 without drawing attention. Amy Andrews, the willowy and top-heavy real estate agent, met her as she walked into the sales office.

"Ms. Braun, it's a pleasure to see you again," Amy's too high voice purred.

Relax, sister, you already got the commission, Michael thought loudly to herself as she handed Amy a note that let her know she was meeting Mr. Fitzpatrick at three.

The information caused a wild panic of activity. Michael, for her part, accepted the espresso made for her and lounged on the creamy leather sofa to wait for Sean.

He arrived fifteen minutes later and was greeted by the staff of The Lofts on La Branch before Michael could even get to her feet. She watched as Sean greeted each of the individuals by name and was impressed with his obvious knowledge of what was going on with the renovations of the building, contracts for pending sales, and Amy's blatant attempt to catch his eye.

"I haven't even said hello to my sister," his deep voice, still with a hint of Ireland, told the now clingy Amy as Sean moved toward her.

"Oh, my god," Sean signed.

"Tell me about it. Who hired her?"

Sean laughed and looked guiltily over his shoulder at Amy's retreating motion. "I did that, but her recommendations were great."

"I bet they were," Michael teased. She moved to her brother and waited as he leaned down to kiss her.

"I'm glad you're here," she told him, taking his hand. "I would say it's been tough, but really with Dan, David, and Kelly, I have been spoiled beyond belief. They have wrapped me in a big bubble of love. I'm just waiting for the damn thing to bust."

Sean shook his head. "Damn, you are cynical. Let's go look at the new digs."

They spent the next hour going from room to room and trying to avoid bumping into the half dozen workers who were working in the penthouse. In fact, the entire building seemed to be swarming with construction workers.

As they explored, Michael described what the decor of each area of the house was going to be. She informed

Sean she was arranging the first floor for herself if she ever moved in and the second floor for guests and Sean when they were in Houston.

Sean approved of her choices, which didn't surprise Michael. They had always had similar tastes; it had been easy for Michael to make the decisions she had made.

They ended their explorations on the roof, where they were able to enjoy the deck furniture that had already been delivered. Doris had already had the landscapers up on the roof, and it was a comfortable friendly place to relax.

"Michael," Sean said, using his voice then switched to ASL.

Michael had been looking over the roof's protective wall when Sean said her name. She turned to face him.

"I know how he found you."

"How?"

Sean looked at Michael and sighed. "Do you remember in January when I was here and you came to the Toyota Center to see me? I thought we were alone, but someone had a camera. They took a photo of us talking. Then, whoever that was, sold it to some fan that has a website about me. The caption with the photo said, 'Sean Fitzpatrick with an unknown woman in Houston, Texas.'"

Michael sat down on one of the chaise lounges. "He knew about the website and made the connection that I was here." She pointed to the roof of the building meaning Houston.

"That's my guess," Sean said. "But what I don't get is why he attacked you then left and hasn't bothered you since.

I mean, you know he's had this thing about you all your life."

Michael shook her head. She had no idea. "Maybe he just had had enough. Maybe he almost got caught, and it scared him enough for him to think about what he's doing." What else could it have been?

"Well, I've done a bit of investigating on my own. He lives in Georgia with his wife and two children. He is very successful in the pharmaceutical business. I can't believe he would risk everything for a thirty-year-old . . . whatever it is." Sean stood up and had started to pace.

Michael watched as Sean's long legs carried him over the vast rooftop. She knew Sean had money, lots of money; suddenly, a thought occurred to her that brought her to her feet.

"Sean," she said, making sure he was looking at her. "I don't want you to do anything stupid. Let's assume he has given up. I'm safe, but you have too much to lose."

"What are you talking about?" Sean asked.

"I mean you could, you have the money, to make him go away, but it's not worth it."

Realization of what Michael was saying flashed across his face. Michael knew she had pissed him off, but she didn't care.

"Oh, you really must think I'm a fucking idiot," Sean said, using his voice.

"No, I just don't want you to do something that could ruin your life. He isn't worth it and really, neither am I."

Sean turned his back to her. She didn't move to touch him but returned to the chaise and sat. Michael glanced at her watch; it was almost six. She had told Dan she would be home around seven and suggested they order pizza for dinner. Being a basketball fan, Michael was certain Dan would freak when he got home and discovered Sean.

"I know what you are trying to say, Michael," Sean said as he walked to where she sat. "I agree, except, you would be worth it. But there are legal ways of dealing with him. Now that we are sure it was he who attacked you, we can get my lawyers involved in such a way that if he sets foot in Texas, his ass is in jail."

"I hope you're right, but we really don't know it was him," Michael told him as Sean pulled her to her feet and toward the stairs.

"I'm as sure as I need to be," Sean replied as they headed down the stairs.

They arrived at the condo at 6:40. They had left the lofts with Sean, poured into Michael's car, and had arrived safely in the garage without anyone the wiser. Michael went up to the third floor to put clean sheets on the large king-size bed and put fresh towels in the bath. While she did this, she practiced ways of telling Dan exactly who her baby brother was. She didn't get the chance.

CHAPTER 30

Dan walked into the house and rounded the corner, stopping dead in his tracks, something that was becoming a habit. Sitting in the living room watching ESPN was an extremely tall and famous basketball player. He looked up when Dan entered the dining room, stood, and was heading Dan's way to greet him; he hoped.

"Hel—" the man started to say before Dan held his hand up to silence him.

"D-d-do you know . . . ah, do you know where my girlfriend is?" Dan stammered.

"Upstairs."

"Thank you," Dan said and shot up the two flights of stairs, calling to Michael. Dan heard Michael whistle, her way of answering back from the master bath. He ran into the bathroom and swooped Michael into his arms, kissing her breathlessly before asking, "Why is Sean Fitzpatrick, the NBA All-Star three years running, that Sean Fitzpatrick, in my living room?"

He watched Michael as she started to laugh, seeing tears roll down her cheeks.

"This isn't funny, and I am serious," he warned her.

"Let's go down so I can introduce you to my big brother. It would only be fair."

Dan sat on the toilet. Michael's brother was *the* Sean Fitzpatrick. "Sweet Jesus," he said out loud.

"No, just Sean," Michael said, getting his attention by tapping his shoulder.

"Very funny." Dan allowed Michael to take his hand and lead him down the stairs to the living room. He felt like an idiot by the time they had reached the last step.

"Sean, I would like to meet my . . . umm . . ."

"Boyfriend," Dan supplied the word Michael seemed to have a problem finding.

"My boyfriend, Daniel Hartman," Michael echoed then stepped back.

Dan reached out and shook Sean's hand. Dan had large hands, but they all but disappeared into Sean's.

"Nice meeting you, Dan."

"Nice to meet you," Dan said, hoping he didn't sound like a total idiot. "I knew Michael had a brother, but I didn't know it was you." He turned to look at Michael who was smiling to herself in the corner of the living room. "You've been holding out on me." Dan waved a finger in her direction. "What other little secrets are you hiding?" His tone was playful, but it had the opposite effect he had intended. The smile slid off her face, and she paled, just for a second. But he had seen it.

"Let's order pizza. I'm starved," Sean said from behind him.

It took ten minutes to agree on the toppings for the pizza and another forty minutes for it to be delivered. They ate at the dining-room table. Sean was generous with his attention to Dan. He had grilled him about the current NBA teams. Sean answered each of Dan's questions with a good-natured ease.

"How is it you are here today and this weekend? I thought you guys had a game," Dan asked as he finished off the last of three pizzas.

"I happen to be on injured reserve for this week, pulled a muscle. It gave me the chance to come and check up on Michael."

Dan noticed how Sean's gaze had gone to Michael all night long. He was concerned about his sister. He admired the fact that this famous star would take the time and check up on sister halfway around the country. He could have just called. Dan had been angry when he had learned that Michael had a brother in the States and hadn't come to check on her in the hospital or after the attack. Dan had said something to David, who had told him he had talked to Michael's brother and told him to stay where he was, that she was fine.

Why hadn't David, or Kelly for that matter, ever told him about Michael's brother? Dan knew neither was a sports fan, but they both knew who he was. He would have to ask about that later.

At nine, Michael informed the men she was tired. Dan asked if she was feeling all right, having noticed she still hadn't recovered since the day before.

Sean kissed Michael good night on the cheek and, slapping Dan on the back, said, "That's okay, Dan here and I are going to go have a few beers. You get some rest. I'll take good care of him."

Dan was too shocked to speak. Michael's smile returned to her face. "Good, but you two be careful," she said and disappeared up the stairs.

"Do you know a good place to have a beer or two?" Sean asked Dan.

Dan knew a wonderful place. "I happen to know a nice Irish pub that has great beer."

"Sounds perfect, I happen to like Irish pubs." The Irish accent in Sean's voice became very thick as he spoke.

Before they left, Dan went to his bedroom to check on Michael.

"Are you having fun?" she asked as he leaned down to kiss her good night.

"You bet I am, and we're going to O'Brian's."

"Well, you'll be popular tomorrow," Michael said. "Just remember he is my family when you are busy showing him off."

"I will, and I love you." Dan kissed her squarely on the mouth, then headed downstairs.

CHAPTER 31

As expected Sean caused quite a lot of excitement when he and Dan entered O'Brian's. Dan was secretly pleased that Carson and Danton were both at the bar when he walked through the door. He was going to have a lot to talk about tomorrow in the precinct.

Dan led the way to where his two coworkers were staring open-mouthed at his guest.

"Carson, Danton, I would like you to meet a friend of mine, Sean Fitzpatrick. Sean, this is Lucas Carson and Chuck Danton." Dan introduced each of the men in turn.

"Nice to meet you both," Sean said, with a practiced ease that Dan admired.

Over the next hour, Dan watched as Sean handled the crowds of people who interrupted them as they drank a few beers. The four men, including Dan, discussed basketball in detail and sports in general. He was not surprised, however, to discover that like his sister, Sean was intelligent, articulate, and respectful of those around him.

Dan was aware Sean didn't have to come to the bar with him. He had beer in the refrigerator, and if that wasn't to Sean's liking, there was a grocery store only a few blocks away. It was as he was listening to Sean and Carson debate some new ruling the league had implemented that Dan realized this was for him. He was sure Michael was behind this in some way. She knew how he was about basketball.

Just one more reason, he told himself; he had fallen for that extraordinary woman.

At ten thirty, Sean made their excuses, saying he was tired from the trip from the West Coast. He shook each man's hand and accepted their business cards, promising they would be his guests next time his team played the Houston Rockets.

"I really appreciate your doing this, Sean," Dan said as they headed for the car. "I know you have to put up with this sorta crap all the time."

"You're welcome," Sean replied simply.

Dan watched as he stopped several yards from Michael's car. Sean had taken the keys off the bar and had insisted on driving. "I know it's late, but I want to show you something downtown. Do you have the time?" Sean asked Dan.

What was he going to say? Sean had taken the time to make him look like some big shot, introducing Dan as a good buddy. He was Michael's brother, and Dan realized he actually had enjoyed Sean's company after the novelty of who he was had worn off.

"Sure," Dan agreed and headed for the passenger side of the small car. He had been amazed when Sean had poured his tall frame into Michael's car in the first place.

The trip from O'Brian's to the old hotel next to Minute Maid Park took only a few minutes. At eleven at night, downtown Houston had very light traffic. Sean parked the car in front of what was obviously a renovation project, one of many going on in Houston.

"Well, this is it," Sean announced as he turned off the car and began to get out.

Dan followed him to the glass front door and watched as he punched in a code then went inside. Dan heard the door lock behind him as he followed and waited next to Sean as a security guard approached.

"Mr. Fitzpatrick," the guard said, sounding pleased to have the late-night guest.

"Mr. Jamal, how are you tonight?" Sean inquired.

Dan was amazed as he watched Sean. He had seen it all night, Sean's ability to make each individual he came into contact with feel as if they were lifelong friends. He understood what a valuable asset that must be for a man in Sean's position.

"Doing fine, Mr. Fitzpatrick. What can I do you for this evening?"

"You just go back and take it easy. My friend Dan and I are going to have a look around. I have the pass codes for all the electronic locks, so we'll be fine. If not, I'll come find you." Sean nodded at Mr. Jamal.

“This is some place,” Dan commented as they headed to a bank of elevators in the center of the marble and glass lobby.

“Yeah, when I heard it was going on the market earlier this year, I jumped at it. When it is finished, it will have four penthouses and twenty two-bedroom, two-and-a-half-bath lofts. We expect the lofts to sell for about three quarters of a million to a million each. The penthouses—these are the private elevators to the penthouse level—sell for over 3 million,” Dan was informed as they stepped into an elevator.

Dan took in the rich woods lining the elevator walls and tried not to show his shock over the cost of the condos. These kinds of rich surroundings were a new experience for him. Although David and Kelly’s house was large, it was still a family home in the suburbs. The elevator gave off a discreet “ding” as it came to a stop and opened.

The foyer was simple yet elegant, with understated colors and decor. Dan followed as Sean led the way to a set of heavy doors that seemed to be carved of redwood. As he walked through the foyer of the penthouse, Dan touched the door only to discover it was steel. He stopped behind Sean and stood in the center of the entrance of the “great room.” The penthouse was in the process of being decorated. The fumes of fresh paint permeated the air.

“What do you think?” Sean asked him as he took in the vastness of what must surely be the living room.

“It’s big” was the only thing Dan could think of saying.

“It’s Michael’s”

Dan stopped midstride and turned to face Sean. Even though he towered over him, Dan glared at him for a full minute before asking, “What the hell did you say?”

“I said, ‘It’s Michael’s.’” Dan noticed a subtle change in Sean’s demeanor. His tone was still friendly, but there was not quite a threat but a determination about him now that hadn’t been there since Dan was introduced.

“What do you mean, Sean?” Dan had decided to play this by ear. This was probably the reason behind the “night out with the guys” that had occurred not long ago. “What is it you have to say to me?”

Dan could see Sean was somewhat surprised at the tone and response to his words. He offered a brief nod to Dan, a way of telling him he understood they had business.

“Dan, I don’t know you, but I only have one sister. I have protected her as long as I can remember.”

“She doesn’t seem to need much protecting right now!” Dan commented. “Where were you on Halloween night?”

Dan’s words reflected his anger. Despite David’s assurance that Sean understood Michael was being taken care of, if Michael had been his sister, nothing could have kept him away.

“I’m not going to go into why I didn’t come. That is between Michael and me.” Sean cleared his throat and continued, “When this building came on the market, I bought it so I could give Michael a safe, secure place to live. I knew she would refuse because she loved her little house. She has a thick Irish skull.”

Dan detected affection and admiration in Sean’s voice.

"When that sadistic bastard burned her house, I offered her a solution, a place to live. I told her if she put down $100,000, I would take care of the balance. I needed a place to stay when I am in Houston. It also offers a place for our grandparents to stay as well. However, I see how she looks at you. It would take more than an act of God to get her away from you."

"You took her money?" Dan was getting angry, not hearing everything that had been said.

"I took her money. It was the only way I could get her to agree. This building has top-of-the-line security, the best I could afford, and I can afford the best. I've invested her money into a portfolio in her name. I don't want her to know about this, and you have to promise me you won't say anything."

Dan looked at his feet for a second and then said, "You have a lot of convincing to do if you want me to keep anything from Michael."

"Fair enough," Sean said and walked to the large pane window that fronted the room. "Michael has been through more shit in her life than both you and I can imagine. I was there with her, but it happened to her. It's not my place to tell you, it's hers. But—"

"She told me about what happen when your father died," Dan informed Sean.

"Well, that is something that started almost the day Michael was born. Because of that she has guarded her heart. With the exception of my mother, our grandparents, David, Kelly, the kids, and I, Michael has let few people into her life. The last man she was involved with really hurt her.

I don't mind telling you if she would have forgiven me, I'd have killed the son of a bitch."

"You know I'm a cop, right?" Dan asked.

"I know you are, but that doesn't mean I don't mean what I am about to say to you. If you aren't man enough to love my sister and treat her like the wonderful woman she is, then get the fuck out of her life."

Dan didn't back down when Sean got in his face.

"What's that supposed to mean?" Dan spat the words out, stepping toward Sean.

"I don't think she could take it if you left her. She'd be lost. She has given to you something she has never given to anyone, her heart. I can see it when she looks at you. I see it when she talks about you. Do you have the balls to stand up for her if she needs you?"

What a fucking asshole, Dan thought. He took a step back, maybe to take a swing, he wasn't sure. He looked at Sean, sizing him up, and a chill ran down his spine.

First, Dan noticed that Sean was terrified. Not for himself but for Michael. Dan didn't understand what was going on here, but he did understand whatever it was, was coming out of fear. The second thing that Dan noticed was Sean was ready to fight. His entire body was tense.

"She won't survive it."

It was the whispered tone, the pure desperation in Sean's voice that stilled Dan for acting rashly.

"Sean," he started, needing to choose his words carefully. Hell, he needed to be honest.

"Sean, I love your sister. I have finally met the woman I want to marry and share my life with. She is so passionate and strong and loving and caring—shit, I am humbled just to be in the same room with her."

Sean started to relax.

"It's as if I have known her all my life. I can't even imagine what my life was like a month ago. She has so completely changed it." It was more than Dan had wanted to say, but he found he couldn't stop.

"Sean, I think you have it wrong. I would go through fire for her. I'd give away everything I have if it would make her happy. I wouldn't survive if she left me. She is . . . she is . . . " Dan couldn't finish. His throat had seized up on him.

"I know," Sean closed the gap between himself and Dan. He reached over and gave Dan's shoulder a squeeze. "I know, but don't make promises you're not strong enough to keep. I just want you to know I will hunt you down and make you wish to God you were dead if you ever, ever hurt my sister."

"I'm not going to hurt your sister. I'm going to marry her," Dan informed Sean.

Sean seemed to consider Dan for a few seconds before commenting, "What about the bastard who attacked her?"

Dan was surprised by the direction Sean had taken. This segue was unexpected, and he could see a fishing expedition coming a mile way. "We don't have any suspects. The fucker didn't leave anything," he told Sean then mumbled under his breath, "not a goddamned thing."

"I just was hoping you had something? You and your friends at the bar seemed to be wound up about something. I just thought it had something to do with Michael and her case," Sean said over his shoulder as he walked to the living-room window.

Dan felt like he should say something to Sean, "We are working on something, but it doesn't have anything to do with Michael. This is between me, you, and the sofa." He nodded toward the leather sofa placed before the panels of windows. "I have this freak that keeps attacking people and then calling to speak to me and discussing the attacks. His last victim was some blind kid. After we had questioned him at the squad house, he got a phone call on his cell."

Dan moved to sit on the sofa; Sean took the matching chair across from him. "It was like the sick bastard had been in the interrogation, he knew what had gone on. He thinks he's smart, but we have him. We went over the surveillance tapes of the squad room to see who was there who shouldn't have been. This small-time PI who often operates on the shady side of the law was in the squad room for no apparent reason. We think he can give us a good lead."

"If you had a lead, would you tell me?" Sean stood up and questioned Dan.

Dan mirrored Sean's movements and looked up at his face. He could see the same shape of Michael's face in his. Dan grinned. "Yeah, Sean, I would."

"Thank you for that," Sean said and left Dan standing in the middle of the living room of his posh penthouse that belonged to Michael. Sean yelled over his shoulder he would be in the lobby waiting when Dan was ready.

CHAPTER 32

The sound of the alarm, signaling someone had entered the penthouse, woke Catfish. He rolled off the cot that was tucked into a corner of the rented office space and moved to the panel of monitors along the wall.

As his eyes focused, the silhouette of a man filled the far left monitor. A moment later, another man much shorter than the first followed behind.

Catfish laughed so hard his sides hurt.

This was better than he could have ever hoped or prayed for. Sean Fitzpatrick had brought Daniel Hartman to the one place where Catfish could watch and listen to every word they had to say.

It had been so easy to set up surveillance equipment in the penthouse. There were dozens of workers coming and going all day long. All Catfish had had to do was wait for the opportunity to present itself.

After he had seen the fan website with Sean pictured with the Abomination, it had been just a matter of time. His man in Houston had done the rest, gathering all the information he needed to complete his life mission.

Then he could return to his family and his life and be the man he always wanted to be but couldn't because it was still alive.

Catfish lit a cigarette and listened to the conversation, relishing each detail.

He had come to think of Hartman as the unluckiest bastard on the face of the earth. He was going to be destroyed; most useful weapons were destroyed when used. Catfish didn't feel sorry for him but didn't really care for the idea of crushing what might have been a decent man. But he had strayed to the wrong side of what was holy.

Catfish was listening now to everything being said. He could almost feel the tension pouring off the two men though the wireless connection. With each confession, from both Daniel and Sean, Catfish's thin-lipped smile broadened. And when he heard Dan's words, "Sean, I think you have it wrong. I wouldn't survive if she left me. She is . . . she is . . .," and saw the helpless expression on his face, Catfish knew it was time.

The smile slid off his face when Dan announced they had discovered his inept helper. Catfish had known sooner or later this connection would have to be severed; he just wasn't prepared to do it so quickly. He would have to leave within the next hour and tie up that loose end. However, every disadvantage could be turned into an advantage. This was another opportunity to be cryptic; to leave a not-so-subtle message for Hartman.

Catfish took the time to make a few notes on the pad next to the monitors. Tomorrow he would make a few calls, put together the package he would be sending to the police station where Daniel worked. Then he picked up the disposable cell phone he had purchased to use when contacting Dudley Wyman.

After Wyman agreed to meet Catfish at Katy Mills Mall in two hours, Catfish made a few more notes and decided to take the opportunity as he drove to the mall to decide just how he was going to kill Michael.

CHAPTER 33

Michael had gotten up with Dan. She had a sinus headache and wasn't in the best of moods. Dan seemed to be out of sorts as well. They mumbled to each other in their own way as Dan readied for work, and she headed to the kitchen for coffee.

When she returned to the bedroom, she went to the bathroom, handed a cup of coffee to Dan, then putting the lid down on the toilet, sat, and sipped her coffee. She wanted to talk to Dan and had discovered she liked to watch him shave and get ready for work.

She could tell by his gruff mood. Sean had done as she had asked him. She wanted Sean to explain to Dan why she had paid for the penthouse. Maybe Dan was worried she would leave. Michael, for her own peace of mind, needed to have a place to go that was safe for her. In this situation, she couldn't run to her best friends, David and Kelly. It would be too awkward.

Dan nicked himself. "Shit!"

Michael steadied herself and touched his arm. Dan turned his gaze to her, and she smiled.

"I'm not going anywhere unless you want me to," she simply said.

Michael watched relief wash over Dan's handsome face.

He pulled her up from her seat and against him. His body was warm against her skin, and when he kissed her, the cool foam of his shaving cream transferred to her face.

"Michael, why didn't you say anything?" Dan asked her as he held on to her.

She couldn't sign because he had pinned her arms to her side. She smiled and looked down drawing his attention to this fact.

"Sorry," he said as he released her arms.

"I didn't know how. I was afraid," Michael confessed. "Sean really wanted me to do this so I would keep an eye on his investment. I really did it to humor him, and besides, I had to reinvest that money from my house or have to pay taxes on it. It was the best situation I could think of. It worked for both of us."

Dan seemed to accept her explanation. Michael searched his face to see if there was something else that was bothering him. Despite her telling him she wasn't leaving, there was something still gnawing at him.

Deciding the best course was to ask, she did.

Dan looked at her for a second before returning to the mirror to finish shaving. He spoke as he shaved, "Your brother is a little protective of you."

It was not quite a statement or a question.

"We had a hard life growing up before we moved to Ireland. And then we had to take care of each other, as well as take care of our mother, even though our grandparents were always near. It wasn't easy for any of us. Now we are here in America, and we are all each other has."

Michael watched as Dan's eyes caught hers in the reflection. "That's not true anymore, Michael. You have me."

She was caught off guard by the anger in his voice. Michael moved against him, putting her lips to his back and reaching around him so her arms were under his.

"I never had that, not really, before," she signed slowly, awkwardly. "This is new for me."

Dan turned around in his place. "Michael, this is new for me too. You're not the only one who feels overwhelmed by what has happened between us."

Michael looked down, not knowing what to say. There was more, but she just didn't know how to say it.

Dan's fingers lifted her chin so their eyes were focused on each other. "Michael, I'm taking off tomorrow, and you and I are getting out of Houston. I'll book us tickets. We'll go to Cancún for a few days. Just you and me, no bad memories, we'll make some new ones just for us."

Michael smiled up at Dan, then rested her cheek against his chest and relaxed.

CHAPTER 34

Her morning was crazy. She had to drive Sean to the Sugar Land Municipal Airport, where his plane was waiting to take him to Kansas City for a game. He wasn't going to be playing, but he had to be there anyway. Michael had told him she and Dan were going to Cancún for the weekend.

Sean kissed her good-bye and promised to return sometime next week.

After standing at the airport until Sean's plane had disappeared into the sky, Michael called Kelly to let them know that Sean had to leave, but the barbecue was still on for tonight.

Michael drove back into Houston and to the Lofts, where she spent an hour checking on the progress of the work being done on the penthouse. It was beginning to look like a home, and she was pleased with that. Michael thought she should invite her mother over from Ireland for the holidays even knowing she wouldn't come. She would have to ask Sean about it. The invitation would include her grandparents as well. It would be nice to spend Christmas together; it had been a long time.

After she was finished with the loft, Michael headed to the market for hamburgers, hot dogs, and the assorted trimmings that accompanied them. She thought to call and invite Ruth Goldman as a way of thanking her for her loving care while she was recuperating from the attack and was pleased when Ruth agreed.

Michael spent the rest of the afternoon cleaning up and getting ready for the evening. It was going to be strange as Michael already thought of David, Kelly, and the triplets as family and they her. Now Dan was part of that dynamic as well.

The thought of this new "family" put a smile on her face and helped banish the fears she had been holding inside.

CHAPTER 35

It was after lunch when Dan finally settled at his desk. He had been on the run all morning long. All hell had broken loose the moment he had set foot at the station. Dudley Wyman had been found murdered, a single bullet to the forehead, shortly after 2:00 a.m. in the parking lot of Katy Mills Mall. It was not lost on anyone in the squad room that this was just a little too coincidental. Somehow, Abomination Guy had known. They discussed the possibility Wyman had been a loose end that had come to the end of his usefulness.

Whatever the reason, it had taken the wind out of their sails. Wyman had been their only possible link between Galvan and Dale.

Carson was sitting at his desk, which faced Dan's. He and Danton had returned from a botched raid on a suspected crack dealer's home, and neither was in a great mood.

Carson's scowling face changed in a second when he asked Dan, "Just how in the hell did you get to be buddies with Sean Fitzpatrick?"

"Easy, I'm sleeping with his sister," Dan commented.

"Holy shit! Michael is Sean Fitzpatrick's sister! Man, how lucky can one guy be. First you're sleeping with one of the hottest women I've seen in a long time—"

"Except your wife?" Garcia added over Dan's shoulder.

"Yeah, whatever, a woman who clearly has the hots for you back. Never happens to most men but then to find out her brother is a professional basketball player. Free tickets, man!" Carson gave Dan the thumbs-up. "Better remember your friends."

"Oh, I'll remember." Dan's phone rang, and he reached for the receiver as he finished his statement. "But it ain't any of you bastards."

They laughed.

"Detective Hartman," Dan spoke into the phone.

"Well, Detective Hartman, finally we speak." The slow Southern drawl was a shock to Dan's system. A chill ran up his spine; somehow he knew it was the Abomination Guy. Both Galvan and Dale had reported that the Abomination Guy had a heavy Southern accent. Now, maybe they could find out where all this was heading. However, deep inside, Dan wasn't sure he wanted to know.

The men standing around him silenced as they noticed the rapid change in his expression. Dan motioned for Carson to pick up the extension.

"I have been waiting for you to call," Dan said in his best detective voice. "You know my name. Can I ask yours?"

The sound of cool laughter reached Dan's ear. Carson motioned for Dan to keep the conversation moving.

"I do believe, detective, that would not be a good idea on my part. I have a mission given to me by the Lord Jesus to complete. But you have been chosen, as I have, to be instrumental in the destruction of this evil."

This man was articulate and intelligent; they were the worst. Dan noticed Carson seemed to be taking notes.

The man continued, "You are being sharpened like a dagger, and I shall point you and drive you into the heart of the beast. The damage you will do, I could never be able to do in all of eternity."

"What do you mean, 'I have been sharpened like a dagger'?" Dan asked, trying to obtain some useful information from this wacko.

"Just as I have said, you will be the instrument that wounds the Abomination so deeply, it will welcome the death I will bring to it." There was laughter on the other end of the phone. Again, Dan felt the hair rise on his arms and neck.

"I don't have any clue what this 'Abomination' is. How am I supposed to be a weapon if I don't know the target?" Dan questioned, thinking to himself, *Give me something you bastard.*

"Well, I see our time to talk is over. But remember, evil often appears in the form of an innocent child or a beautiful woman."

"Wait," Dan shouted into the phone, "what happened to Wyman?"

"Every pawn has a limit to its usefulness, detective. Even your usefulness is limited, effective but limited."

The line went dead.

"Jesus," Carson began as he hung up the line, "he didn't give us shit. We don't know what or who he's talking about. But I am worried about his reference to kids. Crap, do you think he is some sort of serial child molester or something?"

Dan could feel his stomach clench as his thoughts came to his brother.

"Damn, he seems to be targeting me. He appears to be a religious fanatic. I have a brother who is gay and has a husband, and together, they have three beautiful three-year-olds. What if he is talking about them?"

Dan took off toward the back of the station where the profiler had his office. Dr. Patel, for once, was in his office. Dan and Carson gave the new information, including Dudley Wyman's murder, to Patel, who told the men to come back in an hour. He had to finish something he was working on but could get to them at that time.

In the meantime, Dan went to Captain Parker and asked if he still had a tail on Kelly and David. After Dan explained the situation, Parker agreed for the time being to post a plainclothes officer both at the house and at David's office.

An hour later, Dan, Carson, and Parker stood in Dr. Patel's office.

"I don't think he is targeting your family. I'm not sure exactly what he is trying to do here, but you have stumbled onto something you aren't aware of. Has anything different, unusual, or out of place happened in your life, any changes you have made, over the last several months?" Patel asked Dan.

Dan couldn't think of anything and said so.

"Hartman," Carson said, clearing his throat. "Aren't you forgetting something rather important?"

Dan looked at Carson as if he had lost his mind.

"Michael?" Her name was said gently.

"Well, I have a new girlfriend, but that can't be it. Michael, my girlfriend, is a friend of my brother's and his husband. They've know her and I've known about her for eleven years." The thought that this nutcase was after Michael hit too close to home. No one knew she had been assaulted almost a month ago, but it had only been a week or so since this man started contacting Dan.

"He has shown that he is a violent sexual predator, and I felt he was capable of committing murder. Now we know he has done so. His acts of violence are escalating. Were you able to trace that call?"

Captain Parker spoke, "No, he seemed to know how much time he had before that could take place."

"Yeah, he seemed like one smart son of a bitch," Carson commented.

The situation was becoming ridiculous and out of control.

After Patel and the rest of the men had finished discussing what had transpired, Dan returned to his desk and called his brother. He explained the situation and asked if David and Kelly could take the kids and go to Austin or

Dallas or San Antonio for the weekend. Dan confessed he wanted to take Michael away for the weekend but didn't feel he could do that if they were still in Houston.

Dan was relieved when David agreed to pack up the family and head to Dallas for the weekend. David told Dan they had been wanting to go to Dallas to visit with Kelly's parents, and this was the perfect excuse.

David reminded Dan that they were coming to his house for dinner that night and would spend the night and leave early the next morning.

Before Dan hung up, he asked David for a favor.

"Are you sure?" he had asked Dan after Dan had explained to David what he wanted.

"More than you can imagine," Dan admitted.

"Okay, but don't fuck this up," his brother warned.

Great, Dan thought to himself, *even my own brother thinks I'm gonna "fuck" this up.*

Next, he texted Michael to see if there was anything he needed to bring home for dinner and just to touch base. Then he got online and bought two tickets to Cancún and made hotel reservations.

When Dan arrived home that afternoon, he wasn't surprised to learn Sean had left. In a way, he was relieved. He liked the man but hadn't felt as if they had reconciled their conversation the night before. He understood his protective attitude regarding Michael. Dan would do the same for David. However, in all that had been said, something had been left out, and Dan wasn't sure exactly what he had missed.

All Dan could do was to wait and see. He had realized it really didn't matter. This weekend was going to change his life.

That evening, Dan enjoyed having his brother and his family at the condo for a meal. He watched with delight as Michael interacted with the triplets. She was gentle, loving, and at the same time, reinforced boundaries that had been set. For the first time in a very long time, he thought about what it would be like to have a family.

The kids' little fingers and hands communicated with Michael in their native language of ASL. Because all three were deaf, as well as Dan and David's parents and grandparents, David and Kelly had made ASL the first language in their home. They would acquire English as they grew, through captioning on the TV, play dates, and other socialization, but their dads signed.

The meal was casual. Michael had readied hot dogs and hamburgers for Dan to cook over the gas grill built into the range. There were french fries, ranch-style beans, and banana splits for dessert.

They all enjoyed themselves and, for the time being, were relaxed.

Neither Dan nor David mentioned their conversation or why David and Kelly were heading to Dallas in the morning. David and Kelly had packed and would leave from the Stanford Condo first thing in the morning. Dan and Michael's flight left from the intercontinental airport at 9:00 a.m.

At around eight, Kelly and Michael took the kids upstairs to settle them down for the night. Dan and David were sitting in the living room, waiting for their partners to return.

"Did you bring it?" Dan asked. He had waited all evening to ask but hadn't had the chance to be alone with David.

Dan watched as David got up and went to the coat tree. He removed a small brown envelope from his jacket pocket and handed it to Dan, who folded it in half and stuffed it in his jean pocket.

"Are you sure about this?" David's voice held a warning note.

"I told you I am."

"Is this why you're going to Mexico?"

"That and just to get away from all the crap that's happened around here," Dan told his brother.

David moved to stand over Dan, who had sat back down. "I wish you good luck." David offered Dan his hand.

Dan was surprised when he noticed his hand shaking as he took his brother's.

David laughed. "It's about time, baby brother. I'm happy for you."

Dan was pulled up and into David's embrace. He actually was astonished at the strength David had.

"If you're going to have a hug fest, why weren't we invited?" Kelly's voice stated from the end of the couch.

Dan looked up, kissed his brother on the cheek, and stepped away. "Because this was a super secret twin thing that can't be discussed, or we would have to . . . " Dan made a tsking sound as he slowly shook his head from side to side, then finished his comment by adding, "It just wouldn't be pretty."

Kelly laughed and stepped into David's arms. Dan held out his arms for Michael who followed Kelly's example. There were kisses exchanged, and then the four found places to sit and talk.

The topic of conversation for the next hour or so was the penthouse. Dan had told them he might just have to move and live like the other half. His job was to convince Michael to rent him a closet. His reasoning was the closets in the penthouse loft were bigger than most apartments he had rented.

When Dan and Michael were in bed, Dan asked, "Are you excited about our trip?"

She put her warm lips to his and kissed him, her way of saying she was.

Dan lifted a hand. "We are going to have to get up in a few hours just to pack. I know how you women are."

Michael smiled seductively at Dan and signed, "I'm taking a toothbrush, a swimsuit, a pair of shorts and two tops, and a pair of sandals that matches everything. But I plan on wearing what I have on right now for most of the time."

Dan was rewarded with the smooth warm feel of Michael's skin against his as she moved over him.

Oh yes, it was going to be a great weekend.

CHAPTER 36

They had been in the air for an hour. When Dan had gotten up to use the restroom, Michael glanced down at her left hand and at the three-diamond engagement ring encircling her finger and smiled. It certainly had been a wonderful and eventful two and a half days.

Their flight had left Houston's intercontinental airport at nine Saturday morning and arrived in Cancún at a little after eleven. Michael, who had been to Cancún before, was nevertheless very excited when the taxi delivered them to the Royal Solaris Cancun Hotel.

The lobby of the Royal Solaris Cancun was breathtaking, as was the hotel itself. After checking in and getting information on several of the excursion packages the hotel offered, Michael and Dan headed to their room. They followed the bellhop into the elevator and up to the fourth floor, and with quick efficiency, their luggage was deposited into the bedroom, with wide glass sliding doors leading to a balcony overlooking the white sands of the Caribbean.

As Dan tipped the bellhop, Michael stepped out onto the balcony and closed her eyes. She took a deep breath, savoring the flavors of flowers, sea, and aromas of foods carried on the breeze. She heard the door close behind her, and within seconds, Dan's arms encircled her waist.

"Whatcha thinking?" he whispered in her ear.

Signing higher than was natural, Michael leaned her head against his chest and commented, "I was thinking how beautiful it is here and when we were going to go have something to eat."

Dan kissed her neck and rubbed his hips into Michael, showing her all too well his thoughts were not about food. "I thought we might have some dessert before we had lunch," he whispered in her ear.

"What did you have in mind?" Michael asked as she returned the pressure on Dan's full groin.

Without saying anything, Dan's fingers started unbuttoning her silk blouse. Skillfully, he unclasped the front hook of her bra and massaged her nipples to hard peaks. Michael's knees gave as with one hand, he reached inside her slacks and found her center.

His hot breath, his tongue, his lips worked their magic at the base of her neck while each hand pleasured a different part of her.

The orgasm rocked Michael, and she would have fallen to the tiled floor of the balcony if Dan had not held her up with his strong arms. She turned and took his mouth, hungrily kissing him and backing him into the coolness of the room.

It was her turn to work magic on his body. From the balcony to the king-size bed, Michael had rid Dan of his clothes. She shoved him onto the bed, and when he started to speak, Michael lifted a finger to silence him.

Dan closed his eyes. Michael was an incredible lover, and he ached with anticipation. He sucked in harshly as her tongue ran along the inside of his thigh, finding its way to his sacs, tasting and caressing each before she moved to his throbbing shaft.

He ran his fingers through the fine hair that now covered Michael's head. He wished it had been longer so he could wrap his fingers into it.

"Jesus, Michael. Honey, stop!" he pleaded. She was bringing him to the edge; if she didn't stop, he would come. "Oh god!"

In both agony and relief, Michael's mouth felt his shaft and headed up his chest. The feel of her tongue swirling around his navel caused him to suck in his breath, tightening the muscles in his abdomen.

His hands reached for Michael's and pulled her up so he could kiss her. His tongue teased and tasted her, himself, her. He was on fire.

"I need to be inside you," he growled as he fiercely shifted their position.

His hands pinned hers to the down filled comforter, making Michael feel as if she were floating in the clouds. She smiled at that silly thought.

Dan's voice, rough from passion, brought her eyes open. "I'm not finished pulling a smile on your face." With those words, he thrust deep and hard into Michael.

Her body arched into his, her eyes closing again.

"Look at me!"

Michael opened her eyes again and looked into Dan's face. His eyes were dark and hooded, his lips swollen from their devouring kisses. His body was covered in a fine sheen of moisture.

"Look at me!" he said again, his voice both a command and a plea.

Michael stared into his eyes as he began to stoke. His eyes held hers. Even as the tightening, electric chaos began to stir in her center, Michael's eyes didn't waver. When Dan's eyes dilated and his own orgasm hit him, meeting hers, his eyes filled with tears.

"I love you!" The words seemed to be torn from his soul, and Michael's heart broke and mended within a split second of eternity.

Michael wrapped her legs around Dan's waist as he tried to move off her. Shaking her head, she pulled him down on her so his chin nuzzled into her neck. She felt the strong rapid rhythm of his heart, knowing it matched hers.

Michael held up her hand in the ASL equivalent of "I love you." Dan's hand mimicked the sign and touched his hand to hers.

"Baby, I'm too heavy. Let me get up." Dan whispered and carefully lifted his body off Michael's and then moving to his side pulled her in to spoon against him. "I didn't think that sex could get any better, but you amaze me every time. I must be the luckiest son of a bitch in the world."

"You are," Michael teased.

He slapped her bare bottom and nipped her shoulder but couldn't think of a sharp retort and said instead, "If you are going to use me up like this, you are going to have to feed me. I think we should shower, change, and go find something to eat. What'd ya say about that?"

Michael moved away from Dan and onto her back so Dan could see her better. "Let's conserve water and shower together."

Dan laughed as her eyebrows did a quick up and down movement characterized by Groucho Marx. "What a good idea," he said as he rolled off the bed and strolled into the bathroom.

An hour later and almost at the point of sexual exhaustion, Dan and Michael sat down for a very late lunch.

While they ate lunch, Michael and Dan scanned the brochures for each excursion. They discussed each, weighing the pros and cons of which they had done before or not. By the time they were finishing their Bananas Foster, they had decided.

"I think we should take the catamaran excursion that has the lunch and snorkeling on the reefs tomorrow," Dan suggested as he spooned a bit of ice cream into Michael's mouth.

"Okay," Michael bargained, "we'll do that tomorrow morning, and this afternoon at two, we take the rainforest/ Mayan temple tour. I've never seen a Mayan pyramid, have you?"

"No, never a pyramid. However, I have seen an Irish goddess." He leaned over and kissed her.

Michael kissed him back and reached for him under the table. She had turned into a sex fiend, she thought to herself. It was a new and wonderful experience and one Michael didn't want to let go of yet.

"What are you doing?" Dan said against her lips.

She mouthed the word "Nothing."

"Oh, really?"

Michael's hand was moved from his crotch to his lips. She pulled away so she could watch as his tongue played across her knuckles. Dan's eyes drifted to her mouth as it opened in a silent moan.

"If you keep this up," Dan said, as he placed her hand on the table, his still covering her smaller one, "you will never see any pyramid. Your choice."

She rolled her eyes and smiled. She wanted him but wanted to see the pyramids. Michael knew neither would be disappearing anytime soon. Dan would be in her bed for at least another two nights. Having determined she could have Dan in the afternoon or evening, Michael touched Dan's lips with her finger and shrugged her shoulders. "The pyramids it is," she said as she stood up.

Michael lay in the predawn hours and looked over Dan's sleeping form. Despite only having had five hours of sleep, she was not tired. They had returned to the hotel about eight after spending almost six hours exploring the Mayan ruins that were surprisingly near the hotel.

After returning to their room, they showered together, then ate the lukewarm meal they had ordered from room service. Following their meal, Dan had stretched out on the bed. Before Michael could return from the bathroom, he was asleep.

It hadn't bothered her. She quietly moved around the room, turning off the lights, and allowed the room to be bathed in the light of the full moon. Michael watched him sleep, enjoying the rhythmic motion of the rise and fall of his rib cage.

She had followed him after about thirty minutes. Now she was awake.

The little voice in her head that sometimes was relentless in its worries had started long before she was fully awake. It had scolded, warned, chastised, and threatened Michael. She knew she needed to have the "talk." She understood that it was important Dan knew about her past, even as he said it wasn't important.

She had wanted to have that discussion with Dan this morning, but the last thirty-six hours had been so wonderful, how could she possible say or do anything that would devastate the rest of their time in Cancún.

Michael glanced at the clock on the nightstand, six thirty. Their snorkeling excursion didn't start until nine, so what was she going to do for the next two and a half hours? She lay back down and took a deep breath. Dan's arm snaked around her waist, pulling her into his side.

"Go back to sleep," he said to Michael not knowing if he was fully awake himself.

So she did.

CHAPTER 37

The captain of the small cruiser provided a breakfast of fresh fruit and coffee and boxed lunches for later in the day. Michael hadn't been snorkeling in a long time and enjoyed the bright color of the fish and coral. The water, even though it was late November, was warm, and the hours flew by.

When they returned to the hotel around three, they showered and rested. Michael had noticed Dan had begun to get increasingly anxious and suggested he take a nap. He had agreed, but as she drifted off to sleep, she was aware of his getting up, telling her he was going down to the lobby and for her not to get up.

For dinner, Dan had insisted they dress. Michael had packed one nice sundress and noticed Dan had a pressed pair of khakis and a light sports jacket. She hadn't thought anything of it.

They were greeted by a maître d' and taken to a table in the center of the lavish dining room.

"Dan, I really have had a nice time. It's been a long time since I had a vacation and an even longer time since I got to enjoy it with someone as handsome as you. Thank you."

"The pleasure has been all mine," he said as he kissed her fingers.

"You're going to hate going back to work."

Dan didn't respond until the waiter left after delivering their drinks and appetizers.

"Oh, I'll manage somehow."

"Poor baby," Michael signed one-handed as she sipped her margarita.

"I know, you being a woman of leisure, you should feel sorry for me."

"If you want," she teased, "I can go back to work, but I have to tell you, the man I work for is a slave driver."

"I've heard that."

She laughed. "I wish we didn't have to go home tomorrow."

"Well, we could stay longer, but then I would be out of a job, and you would have to go back to that slave driver to support me."

Michael, who had moved from across the table to take a seat next to Dan, leaned over and kissed him. "Any time."

"Shit," Dan cursed, surprising Michael.

"What?"

"I wanted to wait until we had finished dinner, but I can't."

Michael looked at him not knowing what he was talking about. She looked around the restaurant, trying to see if there were any clues as to what Dan was talking about. When she focused her attention back on Dan, he had gotten out of his chair and had placed himself on one knee at her feet.

Michael's hands went to her mouth, and she stared at him. Could he be doing what it looked like?

"Michael," he started, reaching into the inner pocket of his jacket and removed a small box, "I know we haven't known each other long, but it doesn't matter."

Michael looked at him yet was aware the restaurant had quieted. She could feel the other diner's eyes on them.

"I think I fell in love with you with the first time I saw you. I know that might seem a little twisted considering, but I can't imagine my life without you."

Michael watched as his shaking hands moved toward her, taking her left hand in his. His voice was as unsteady as his hands as he continued, "I don't want a life without you. Michael Hannah Braun, will you marry me?"

Michael looked at him, watching as in slow motion, he slid an engagement ring onto her finger.

"Yes," she mouthed, not wanting to remove her hand from his.

"She said, 'Yes'!" Dan announced to the captive audience.

There was a burst of applause then congratulations as Michael was pulled to her feet and kissed almost senseless.

The rest of the meal had been a blur. Michael carried on a conversation with Dan but hadn't remembered what it was they discussed. As they left the restaurant, they were congratulated with a standing ovation as they passed the other diners.

Michael was still in a daze when she crawled into bed. She had so many things she needed to tell him. The same reason she hid the fact she was Sean Fitzpatrick's sister now would concern Dan. Her childhood, her past, Dan deserved to know.

How was she going to open up a past that was confusing, tragic, and to some, horrible? All Michael had wanted to do was keep that door closed. But she couldn't be the wife Dan deserved if she didn't tell him everything about when she was seventeen, everything that came before.

"You can thank David for that beautiful ring when we get home." Dan had returned from the restroom and had taken his seat next to Michael. "Because he was the firstborn son, our grandmother's ring went to him. Needless to say, Kelly wasn't going to be wearing it. David had it in his safe and brought it to me Friday."

"I will, but remember you told me we could keep this to ourselves for the rest of the week. I want to tell my mother, grandparents, and Sean first," Michael reminded Dan. She had begged him the night before not to tell anyone until she was ready. It would save him the embarrassment of having to announce the engagement was off if, after he had learned about her childhood, he pulled away. It had happened before; she was sure it would happen again.

"Well, David and Kelly already know." Dan took her hand.

"I know, but they're different." Michael couldn't think of anything else to say regarding David and Kelly.

"Baby, I love you. That's really all that matters," Dan assured her.

She hoped it was true!

They had finished making love and Dan had wrapped himself around Michael. She was slowly getting her breath and heart rate back to normal. She was sure of two things; she had never had a lover like Dan nor had she ever been treated as a friend, a confidant, or a lover as Dan had treated her.

He always told her what was on his mind, even when, on the few occasions since they met, he was angry with her. They had been able to discuss their problems or disagreements and resolve them.

As for herself, Michael was able to treat him in the same manner. There was such an ease with their relationship. It was a totally new experience for her and was the reason she had told him yes when Dan had asked her to marry him.

"Dan." She tapped his shoulder and sat up looking him in the face. "I want you to know about my childhood."

It had taken all the courage she possessed just to sign those words.

"I know all I need to know," Dan informed her as he leaned over to kiss her. "I don't care what happened when you were seventeen. That was a lifetime ago."

She agreed, "Yes, it was, but there is more, and I think you should know everything."

Before she could continue, Dan took her back in his arms, pulling her so her back was against his chest.

"Listen," Dan spoke softly in her ear, "I don't care what happened. I love you, just the way you are. You cannot tell me anything to change my mind. Michael, you are the love of my life."

She couldn't speak. She didn't know what she could say. There was more that Dan needed to know, but maybe tonight wasn't the night. They had spent a wonderful weekend in Cancún, had gotten engaged, and had just spent time relating to each other in the most private of ways. How could she tell him now?

Dan continued, "Michael, all I need to know is that you love me and I love you. You have been a part of my family, at least as far as David is concerned, since you were what, nineteen? I don't think there is anything you could say to change any of those facts."

"I do love you," Michael stressed. "I have known David since I was really eighteen, but—"

He gently reached out and took her hands, gently and effectively silencing her.

"I want you to go to sleep and not worry about something that can't be changed. The woman I love is a result of all the things that happened to her since the day she was born. And look what I get, a beautiful, exotic, intelligent woman whom I love more than life."

Michael kissed him. She couldn't stand for him to say another word. She knew how people reacted to people like her, those who had experienced what Michael had experienced.

It very seldom was in a positive way.

CHAPTER 38

Tuesday morning, Catfish smiled and looked around the room. The monitors showed the workers already swarming over the penthouse. He had already chosen his place to wait.

"It starts now." He spoke the words to himself.

CHAPTER 39

"What the hell happened to you?" Carson began to tease Dan as soon as he entered the squad room.

"Yeah," Garcia chimed in, "you have a better tan than I do."

"I took Michael to Cancún for the weekend." There was no point not telling the three men standing around him. Dan had known them long enough to know they would hound him for days to get the information they wanted, which was what made them good cops.

"Hey, Garcia," Danton chimed in, "do you notice a 'stupid man lost to the world' expression on his face?"

"I do," Garcia agreed, moving closer to Dan, effectively getting into his face.

"You didn't! You've only known her a month!" Carson said.

"Didn't what?" Dan asked the trio. He hoped his innocent "I don't have a clue what the hell you're talking about" look on his face worked. It didn't.

"Well," Carson continued, "since you didn't come back to work with your tail between your sorry legs, I assume Michael said yes."

Damn, Dan thought, *these guys were good.* Dan couldn't help himself; the grin he felt spreading over his face must have had him looking like an absolute idiot.

"I'll be damned," Danton remarked.

That was followed by a round of excessive backslapping and congratulations. Dan sure hoped that Michael didn't make one of her impromptu visits anytime soon. She would have a fit because of the reactions she was sure to receive.

Captain Parker interrupted the congratulatory gathering. Once he found out what it was about, he added his well-wishes to those of Carson, Garcia, and Danton.

"I hate to break this up, but I need Hartman to go to the South Houston station. They have an assault suspect there who needs a good interrogation in sign language. You boys can continue this lovefest later." Parker quietly wished Dan congratulations again and left.

Dan took a few minutes to look over his desk to see if anything needed to be handed off before he headed out. Not finding anything that needed immediate attention, Dan grabbed his jacket and headed for the door.

Before he had made it halfway across the room, Garcia waved a thick manila envelope in the air and yelled, "This came in yesterday. It's marked urgent and addressed to you."

Dan stopped for a moment. "It can wait until I get back, just throw it on my desk."

The questioning of the suspect in South Houston took several hours. Along with Dan, three other officers were present in the room. In the end, it was determined the assailant had acted in self-defense and was released.

On the way back to his precinct, the traffic on I-45 had come to a standstill. Dan took the opportunity to use his iPhone to text Michael. While it wasn't very practical to type while driving, the traffic was at a dead standstill.

"What's up," he typed.

"Nothing. Have been cleaning." Michael's response appeared on the small LED screen. "What about u?"

"Stuck in traffic I-45," Dan typed. The blasting of a horn behind him made him look up. The car in front of him had moved ahead three feet. The asshole behind him obviously thought it was Dan's obligation to do accordingly.

"Sorry. What time u b home?"

"Not late, see u soon. Luv, Dan." Dan disconnected the communication as the traffic miraculously began to move again.

Michael put her iPhone on the table and returned her attention to Kelly. Kelly had been at the front door at ten in the morning, claiming David had confessed to giving Dan their grandmother's engagement ring. Although Michael wanted to be upset, she couldn't do it.

She was soon caught up in the excitement Kelly was creating.

"Well, you have to get married in the spring. I mean, before the end of April, otherwise, it's too damn hot. Ooh, ooh, David can give you away. Well, I know Sean should really be the one to do that, but it would be so cool to have the handsome twin of your handsome fiancé give you to him." Kelly's laughter was contagious.

Michael joined in. "It was so romantic," she began and told Kelly the details of the evening right down to the restaurant manager picking up the tab for the meal.

"What about later?" Kelly queried, wiggling his red eyebrows sinisterly.

For lunch, she had whipped up salads, and they continued to plan for the "big event." As Michael listened and commented on what was being said, she sent a prayer to whoever was listening. *Let there actually be a wedding.*

CHAPTER 40

Catfish had packed a duffle bag with the tool he would use. After lunch, he headed over to the Lofts, wearing a uniform of one of the many companies working in the building. No one stopped him or even gave him a second glance.

Within twenty minutes of entering the Lofts of La Branch Street, Catfish was hidden away. From his vantage point, he could see the layout of the penthouse living room; no one could see him.

He smiled. *What to do first,* he thought silently.

CHAPTER 41

Dan was again bombarded with work the moment he returned to the station. A case that he, Carson, and Garcia had been working on unexpectedly broke. Most of what he had to do was done in either an interrogation room or at his desk.

He glanced at the manila envelope for a second and shoved it to the side before making several phone calls connected to the case. The conversations were interrupted by Parker and Garcia, but eventually after an hour, Dan was able to hang up the phone and take a breath.

Again he looked at the envelope. Dan wanted to reach over and throw it in the trash. For some reason just having it on his desk made him feel sick. And it was then, understanding he actually feared what was in it, Dan decided to open it up.

Once he had it in his hands, Dan stared at it as if it were a living, breathing thing. He understood there was a chance it was from the Abomination Guy.

"Get a grip, man," he said to himself.

Taking a breath, Dan reached for his letter opener, a gift from his parents, and sliced open the end.

Looking around to see if anyone was standing around him and finding he was alone, Dan emptied the contents on his desk and felt a hand tighten around his heart.

A photo and a copy of a magazine article fell onto the desk. The photo was of a young teenage Michael and across the front, written in the same hand as the envelope, was "Abomination." The letters were large, red, and seemed to burn into Dan's retinas.

The article, Dan noticed, was a reproduction from the *British Journal of Medicine* publication dated almost twelve years before. As Dan read the article, he began to feel sick. But the sick feeling was quickly being overtaken by a sense of betrayal, humiliation, and rage. By the time he had finished the three pages, Dan could taste the bile rising in his throat.

Dan shoved the envelope and its contents into the bottom desk draw, ran to the men's room, and threw up. First, his lunch, then his breakfast came up, until there was nothing but dry heaves.

Carson, who must have seen Dan's dash to the restroom, came in, and checked up on him as he was washing his face. "Jesus Christ, you look like shit."

Dan could only look at him. The thought of opening his mouth to speak was beyond his power. He looked at his ashen face in the mirror. Dan wanted to yell, to hurt something, someone, to make them feel like he did.

"Must have eaten something in Mexico that didn't set well," Carson consoled Dan.

"Yeah" was all Dan could say. He could feel the rage building and knew he had to put it where it belonged. "I have to go!"

Behind him, Dan heard Carson tell him to take care of himself and get some rest. That wasn't going to happen. Dan paused long enough at his desk to retrieve the envelope and its contents before fleeing out of the station and into his car.

As he drove, a running dialogue played in his head. After reading the article, Dan swore he could hear the click-click of pieces of a puzzle falling into place.

"That's what she was trying to tell you," one voice said in his head.

"She lied, she used you. How does it feel to be a fucking idiot?" the opposing voice commented.

Dan slammed his fists on the steering wheel of the car and screamed. He didn't feel the pain; even if he had, he wouldn't have cared. All he could feel was rage.

The first voice began again, "It doesn't matter."

"The hell it doesn't," the second voice argued. "All this time and you thought you had found the perfect woman. What a fucking joke."

The conversation continued. The second, the injured party, Dan's emotional self, was very convincing. So convincing in fact, by the time he screeched into the front of the house, the rage was in control.

Dan took a minute to breathe before inserting the key into the deadbolt.

The calming voice warned, “Don’t do anything you’re going to regret.”

Out loud Dan said, “I won’t kill the lying bitch, if that’s what you mean.”

Dan closed the door behind him and with all the confusion, betrayal, and the feeling of a wounded animal, yelled, “MICHAEL!”

The dagger had been honed to a deadly edge.

CHAPTER 42

Upstairs in the bedroom they had shared, Michael froze. The sound Dan made when he screamed her name, Michael had heard before. She steeled herself for what she knew was about to happen. She looked around, trying to see if there was a way to escape the room. There wasn't, so she moved from the wall and positioned herself between the bed and the top of the stairs.

She could almost feel the rage emanating from Dan before he entered the room.

"I got something for you," he sneered at her at the same time thrusting a large envelope into her chest with such force Michael flew to the bed.

Michael didn't take her eyes away from Dan's face. It was red from anger and twisted into a mask she didn't recognize. What she did recognize was the handiwork beneath the emotions. Michael started to get up off the bed.

"I don't think that's a good idea," Dan warned her in a deadly calm voice.

Michael got to her knees on the bed and pulled out the contents of the envelope. She recognized at once the photo of herself with the word, that horrible word, covering the front as well as the article. Michael hadn't wanted her grandparents to do that article, but they had insisted, telling their seventeen-year-old granddaughter it was for the best. Maybe it could help some other parent understand what their child was going through.

"I tried to tell—"

"SHUT UP!" Dan interrupted her, spitting the words out of his mouth. "You lied to me. You used me."

The accusation in those words stung as if he had slapped her.

"I told you to stay where you were."

"I didn't lie or use you, I love you," Michael tried to reason with Dan. But that was the wrong thing to say.

Before she realized what was happening, Dan had yanked her to her feet and had her pinned to the wall, his forearm tight against her chest. "Don't you say that? How many other poor bastards have you fucked with? How many have you destroyed with your lies?"

Michael felt the spittle hit her face. It was that moment when she could feel her heart break. It was unbearable, and the tears welled up in her eyes and began to fall.

"Oh, don't cry." Again the warning in Dan's voice was dangerous. "I don't believe you have the balls to cry to my face." Dan laughed a humorless laugh and punched his fist through the wall next to Michael's ear.

She flinched but couldn't move.

With so much pain, hate, and sarcasm as one voice could contain, Dan said, "Of course, you don't have the balls, YOU FUCKING FREAK." He yelled the last words into her face.

She pushed him off her and was suddenly extremely calm. She looked at him for a moment before drawing back and slapping Dan hard across the face then searched his brown eyes for anything she could recognize.

"Freak," Dan mouthed the words.

Michael slapped him again. "I'm not a freak." Michael signed each word. "I-AM-NOT-A-FREAK." She thrust her hand in Dan's face.

"Get out of my house," Dan said as he walked over to the bed to retrieve the envelope. He headed down the stairs but came back into the room, pinning her against the wall again.

Michael watched as he took her left hand and removed the engagement ring roughly from her finger.

Then he left.

CHAPTER 43

David was with a patient when a nurse came in, "Dr. Hartman, can I speak with you for a moment."

David walked out of the examination room and into the hall. "What is it, Rhonda?" he asked.

"Your brother called and said he will be here in about ten minutes. He sounded very angry and upset. I mean I think he was crying. He told me to tell you he had to talk with you, it was important." Rhonda looked nervously at David.

"Is Dr. Fineberg booked solid today?" David asked.

Rhonda didn't know but would find out, she told him. "Okay, ask if he can finish up with my patients until I am done with my brother. I'm almost finished with Mr. Lambert. If Dan arrives before I am finished, tell him to wait in my office."

It took fifteen minutes to conclude the examination of Mr. Lambert and write a prescription as well as explain the proper way of taking the meds. When he was done, David was informed Dan was waiting.

"Oh man, Dr. Hartman," Rhonda warned, "he looks awful."

David was beginning to worry. If something had happened to their parents, David would have already known. This was something different. David could never remember a time when Dan had come to the office to talk to him.

David opened the door and was horrified at the condition he discovered his brother in.

"For god's sake, Dan, what happened?"

Dan, who was almost invisible in the leather chair he sat in, handed David the envelope but didn't utter a word.

"Do you want me to read this?" David inquired as he sat at his desk and pulled out the four sheets of paper. Like Dan and Michael before him, he found a photo of Michael and a twelve-year-old article from the *British Journal of Medicine*. David began to read.

The article discussed a seventeen-year-old Irish American whom they dubbed MHF, who lived in Ireland with a sibling. The child's mother was an Irish citizen and the daughter of prominent physicians in their respective medical fields in Ireland. The child, who had been born genetically a male, had begun showing signs of gender confusion as early as age two. At age of three, almost four, the child had announced he was a girl and refused to do anything that was boyish. Until this time, the boy and his family had lived in America with their father, an American physician.

The child, who was extremely intelligent and functioned in an emotional age of a child several years older, was examined by a psychologist and other physicians who were experts in the field of transgender studies. Almost unanimously they agreed the child fit into the classic criteria for such individuals.

The parents agreed to let the child live as a girl, the father, sure it was a phase that his son would outgrow, the mother, just wanting her child to be happy.

By the time the child was five, the relationship of the parents had fallen apart and the mother divorced their father and moved with her two children back to Ireland.

At the age of ten, her mother as well as her grandparents had petitioned and won the right to begin, on her "daughter's" behalf, hormone treatments that would stave off the secondary masculine maturation and begin the feminizing of MHF.

MHF reported every six months to a team of physicians, a psychologist and other therapist (all who had written the article) until MHF was sixteen. Just after MHF's sixteenth birthday, gender reassignment surgery was performed, changing MHF's male genitalia to female. Additionally, her birth certificate was changed to reflect the change in gender.

The article went on to say MHF was not an unusual case and was typical of individuals with gender identity disorder. A footnote informed the readers that MHF was considering returning to America to attend college.

David put the papers on his desk and looked at his twin. “Are you okay?” he asked.

“What do you think?” Dan’s voice was cold and bitter. “Did you know about this?”

David looked at his brother, gauging his emotional state. “No.”

David watched as his brother’s body stiffened with anger. “That fucking freak! I can’t believe I got involved with that . . . that . . . thing! She lied to me, David. I gave her my heart, asked her to marry me, and she lied to me. Jesus Christ, I fucked her.”

David had become angry with every word his brother had uttered. He had known Michael since she was eighteen. Had never known her as anyone other than this beautiful loving friend, this beautiful woman.

“Shut up,” David told Dan in a steely tone.

Dan looked up at David with surprise. “What did you say?”

David stood up and punched his brother hard across the jaw. “I said, shut up!”

It was David’s turn to be enraged. “I can’t believe you called Michael a ‘fucking freak.’ You don’t get to choose who you fall in love with, not really, not ever! No one does!”

David shoved Dan back into the chair when he tried to stand up. He moved over his brother, and with his knee in Dan’s crotch and his weight pinning Dan’s arms to the chair, he continued to say through clinched teeth, “You love her. *Her!* You asked *her* to marry you. It doesn’t matter how she was born. You don’t get the chance to meet someone who changes your life but once maybe twice in your lifetime.

So what, if she wasn't born a girl, she grew up to be a wonderful, loving woman."

David bounced his weight on Dan's arms, making him moan in pain. "Do you think I wasn't surprised when I met and fell in love with Kelly? Do you think I didn't wonder if I was throwing my career away by coming out of the closet and telling the world I was in love with that wonderful man? Do you? Don't you, for one minute, think it would be easier for me professionally if Kelly had a cunt instead of a dick?" David moved away from Dan taking a devious pleasure out of the wince Dan gave at his words. "You're a fucking idiot!" He seethed.

David was unaware his voice had risen almost to a shout until Rhonda opened his office door. "We're having a family discussion, Rhonda. Close the door and don't let anyone in."

David returned his attention to his obviously very stupid brother. "Well, I did. But I didn't care. I love that man. I love him more than anything but our kids."

"That's different, you're gay," Dan said, seeming to find his voice.

David punched him again. "But Michael isn't. Neither are you and you had better get your shit together and realize what you have before you throw it away. I want to ask you a question."

David stepped farther away from Dan but warned him to stay in his seat.

"How many women have you screwed in your lifetime?" David asked bluntly.

"That's none of your fucking business?" Dan glared at him.

"Cut the crap and answer the question. With all the women you have slept with and then with Michael, did you notice a difference?"

David watched as Dan considered the question then shook his head no. "And your buddies at the station, have they met Michael?"

Dan nodded yes, seemingly unsure where David was heading with his questions.

"Oh, I see, and they all said, 'Gee, Hartman, I see that beautiful woman you're boning was a boy for about the first four or five years of her life.' Is that it?"

"Don't be stupid," Dan said, squirming in the chair.

"That's what I'm telling you, little brother. 'Don't be stupid.'" David's anger had changed now into pity. Straight people were so clueless most of the time. When all that really mattered was that someone loved you and you loved them back, he told his bother as much.

David watched as all the bravado Dan had carried into the room melted away. He seemed to shrink in on himself, and for the first time, David saw fear, then tears.

David took his brother in his arms as he began to sob violently. David did what he could to soothe him. He understood he was hurting. After a few minutes, David inquired, "Are you going to be able to go home and have a calm conversation with Michael about all this? She didn't do anything to you. She didn't lie, and I know for a fact she loves you and you love her. Just remember the last time the two of you made love. Michael is still that wonderfully passionate woman you told me touched your soul."

Dan extended his hand, and David was almost sick with what he saw when Dan opened his fist, the engagement ring.

"Oh my god, tell me you didn't go home before you came here?" David pleaded.

He watched in horror as Dan's head fell to his chest.

"What did you say?"

Dan looked up, and David saw in his brother's eyes all he needed to know. It was time to be concerned for Michael. "What did you say?" David asked again.

"I was cruel."

"Why didn't you just drive a knife into her heart, you stupid asshole. You might as well have . . . " David would have said more, but the expression on Dan's face stopped him cold.

"What?" he asked.

Dan told David about the phone call from the man who sent the article and photo. David knew some of the information, which was why he had agreed to go to Dallas for the weekend before. However, when Dan had told him the man had told Dan he would use him like a dagger in the heart of the Abomination, it was David's turn to sink into a chair.

"And you did, you might as well have used that fucking dagger," David accused in a whisper.

"I have to find her." David watched as Dan was overcome with a panic and raced out of the room.

David thought, *I hope for his sake nothing happens to Michael. He won't be able to live with himself if she gets hurt.*

As soon as Dan was in the parking lot, he made two phone calls and then headed to his condo. "God," he spoke out loud, "please let Michael know I was a stupid asshole and didn't mean anything I said. Please let her be safe."

CHAPTER 44

At 5:10, the November sky was already almost dark. The lights from Minute Maid Park cast a bright glow throughout the penthouse but especially the living room with its two-story banks of windows. Catfish enjoyed a coke and a sandwich as he waited.

By five thirty, Catfish was reading from his pocket New Testament in an attempt to get into the correct mood for what he would be doing soon, he hoped. He didn't have to wait long.

How appropriate, Catfish thought to himself as the elevator chime announced the arrival of someone, that the radiant hands on his Rolex declared it was 5:56. The devil had arrived.

From his vantage point, Catfish watched with growing satisfaction as the Abomination entered the living room. It threw a small duffle bag across the empty room, and as if its bones had miraculously dissolved, the creature collapsed to the floor. Catfish watched as it opened its mouth and attempted to scream.

A chill ran up Catfish's spine. The silence of its scream was as loud as ten foghorns. But a thin-lipped smile bisected his face. Oh, he had done a good job in sharpening Daniel Hartman to use as his weapon. The wound appeared to be deep and possibly lethal. It was time to find out.

He moved silently from his hiding place on the second floor until he stood within a foot of the Abomination. He waited until he was sure it was aware of him.

"Well, baby nephew, oh sorry, niece, I think it is all going to end here," Catfish told the Abomination.

Slowly, it turned its face to him. It didn't try to remove the tears that ran down its face.

"I have waited a long time for this," Catfish said as he struck the creature in the face with the back of his hand. He noticed it stared at him but didn't back away.

He reached for an arm and yanked it to its feet. "You understand why I can't allow you to live?" he asked not really expecting an answer.

It moved its hands about, waving them in the air like some spastic four-year-old. Catfish understood it was trying to communicate. They had tried to teach him this language, but he hadn't wanted to learn and never did.

"I don't understand you. It's only necessary for you to understand me." He wasn't sure exactly what he was trying to explain, but maybe it was God's will.

To his surprise, it gave him the bird and moved so quickly Catfish could not evade the elbow that found his chin. He fell back and hit the floor.

It had some fight in it after all.

Catfish caught the collar of its shirt as it attempted to reach the stairs. With a forceful tug, it flew backward and slid across the polished oak floor. He was on it before it could move.

"You think you can get away from me this time? Well, you're wrong. I have waited for almost thirty years to do this, and I will finish it tonight." Catfish ran his hand over its breasts. It slapped at him and received another well-placed blow to its face. Catfish wiped the blood that had stained his hand on its torn shirt.

"I want you to know why I'm doing this. I want you to know how you destroyed my father's life, how you ruined mine." He would have grabbed it by the hair, but it was still too short to get a hold of, so he took hold of an arm again and pulled it to its feet.

"You took my father from me, you and your slut of a mother," he yelled as he dragged it up to the second floor. Every few steps, Catfish delivered a slap or a blow. However, at the top of the stairs, he received a punch to the head that fueled his anger.

"So you have some fight in you after all. When you were seventeen and new, you didn't have much fight. I took your virginity from you. It was only fitting. And to think," Catfish said, smiling into the bloodied face looking back at him, "I am going to be the last one to fuck you as you die. How does that sound?"

At the top of the stairs, he pushed the Abomination to the floor and sat on its' back. Reaching into his duffle bag, he found the duct tape and used it to tie its hands behind its back.

"Do you remember that afternoon you, I, and Billy Ray Jones spent together? I still remember. I seem to recall I left you with a reminder or two." Having said that, he got an idea and reached for a hunting knife in his bag. Catfish used it to cut away the flannel shirt it was wearing.

Having finished cutting away the shirt, he looked at its' back. "I see you still have the reminders, how sweet of you."

He ran his tongue over several of the raised ridges before he flipped it over on its back. He looked down at its chest, the lacy bra offering up the well-shaped breasts like sacrifices to the gods. Catfish noticed a thin pink line from where a piece of glass in the garage had cut into its flesh. He traced the line of the scar and dipped under the soft material with his fingers trying to tease the nipple.

Oh, how nice and soft it was. He placed his mouth on the tip of its breast. It bucked trying to get him to stop. Bitch! Catfish took its face in his hand. "You don't deserve to live. I was fine until you came along."

He remembered the night at the church when his brother had brought the newborn baby for everyone to see.

"My daddy said you were the most beautiful baby he had ever seen. And you know, you were. But then you were so different. You had them unnatural colored eyes, you didn't make a sound. I could have almost lived with that even though my father told me you would be evil."

Catfish pulled it up again to its feet and dragged it back down the stairs along with the duffle bag.

Next he used the knife to cut away its jeans. It tried to move.

"I'd stop that if I were you. You know how dangerous knives can be." To drive his point home, Catfish stuck the tip of the knife an inch or so into the Abomination's thigh.

"Oh, did I hurt you?" he asked as he finished cutting the jeans. "Are you feeling a bit humiliated yet? A little embarrassed? Don't worry, you will, when they find your naked body with a beautiful and informative sign around your dead neck, you will."

"I remember when you were about four and you were playing outside with the neighbor girls. I looked out there and you had that black curly hair, and you looked at me and smiled. You know that day, I understood. It was right before you told everyone you were a girl and not a boy."

Catfish looked at Michael, really looked at her.

"You looked just like your mama. She was beautiful. My brother loved her so much, but you ruined that. Your mama talked him into taking you to all them fancy doctors, and when they got home, I remember him telling me and Sean, you weren't a little boy but a girl."

"He should have hated you for that, but he just loved you more. I hated you. I hated you 'cause I could see you, the real you. I tried to make them see how evil you were, but that bitch of a mother of yours didn't listen to me. She divorced my brother and packed you and Sean up and planned to move back to Ireland."

Catfish slapped her again. How he hated her! Catfish was unaware that his mind had begun to shift from "it" to "her"; he understood that the devil had made a temptress.

"My brother grieved. And every time your mama sent school photos of you and Sean, he'd say, "Look at my beautiful daughter and handsome son." But, goddammit, I was his baby brother. I was first, but you took that away from me. He couldn't protect me 'cause he was grieving over *you*!" Catfish screamed into her face.

"Even on his deathbed, he asked for you. I was standing there, and he asked for you," Catfish was shouting now. All the hurt and anger welled up to this moment.

Michael was fighting to get away from Catfish. He let her move a few feet away before he asked, "How do you want to die?"

Michael moved her mouth.

"Oh, you're going to die," Catfish leaned over so his thin lips were only inches for Michael's, "tonight." He glared into her eyes, then with a sickening smile, extended his tongue and flicked the tip over Michaels' trembling mouth.

Catfish pulled away and continued conversationally, "It could be slow or fast. I could strangle the life out of you as I fuck you or fillet you like a trout. Of course, you know I am going to rape you before I kill you. You deserve it." He slapped her hard across the face.

For the first time, Catfish saw panic in Michael's violet eyes. That brought a smile to his face. He stood up to open his duffle bag, watching as she scrambled away from him.

"I have a gun," he informed her, "maybe just one bullet between those lovely eyes of yours. But you know I want a little something to remember you by before you leave. I brought a few toys I thought you might enjoy."

Michael was moving farther away from him, but he didn't really mind. The hunt, the chase, was as important and satisfying as the sex would be. In fact, a little roughness could only spice things up a bit.

Catfish waited until Michael had gotten to her feet and was running before he began the chase.

"Oh, daughter of my brother, I'm coming to kill you," Catfish teased.

He would let her run. It didn't matter. There were only three ways out of the penthouse: the elevator, the fire escape, and the roof. Catfish would take a moment to block the front door, the only way to the elevator, and he had already fixed the fire escape so that way was barred. This left only the penthouse and the roof. And the roof was where he wanted Michael to go.

He had sent the elevator car back to the first floor. He was unable to disable the elevator in a way that would still allow him to leave after he was finished. Catfish returned to the duffle bag, removed a gun, and a length of cord before going after Michael.

She was easy to follow primarily because she had left a trail. She had somehow removed the duct tape from her wrists. This would make her a little more dangerous, but Catfish was certain he would be able to overpower her.

Catfish took to the stairs, which is where he discovered the tape. The penthouse, though large, was mostly open in its floor plan. There were many places to hide, but he had all night. Going from room to room he searched.

"You know, Michael," Catfish spoke loudly, making sure he could be heard, "the longer you keep this up, the rougher I'm going to be in the end although that works for me."

A movement to his right caught his attention. He ducked just as Michael swung a two-by-four at his head. It missed his head, but before he could regain his position, she was able to knock the wind out of his lungs with a powerful swing that connected with his midsection.

Catfish smiled to himself as he tried to fill his lungs with air. He straightened himself and pulled the gun from his pocket and took aim. He waited until Michael was on the third step from the bottom and fired.

His father would have been proud of his marksmanship. The bullet went into and exited from the fleshy part of Michael's right thigh, and Catfish watched her as she tumbled down the remaining stairs.

"Goodness, that must have hurt," he announced from the top of the stairs with his thick twang. She looked up at him, panic in her pale face, and to his amazement, got to her feet and headed toward the kitchen.

"Go ahead. I'm right behind you."

Catfish was really enjoying this little game. It was really too bad it would have to end soon. It had become easy to track Michael now as a trail of blood on the expensive wooden floor and bloody handprints on the wall were visible even in the darkened rooms.

"You know, all I wanted was for you to be nice to me. I wanted to know what it was about you that made my brother love you more than me." Catfish spoke the words not really aware he was speaking out loud or even if Michael was hearing him.

The blood trailed through the kitchen and, as he had hoped, headed into the small anteroom that led to either the fire escape or the roof. Catfish noticed the amount of blood was increasing. He assumed Michael's heart was pumping much faster than normal. Oh, he had better hurry and finish this before she bled out. He wasn't going to fuck a dead body. But maybe he would. The final humiliation!

She had tried to open the fire escape door. The door was covered with blood as if she had tried to break it down to get through. Catfish was surprised as he began to feel admiration for her determination, mixed with the hate and sexual excitement that was increasing as he got closer.

When he stepped out onto the roof, Michael was leaning against the outdoor kitchen counter. Her eerie-colored eyes glared at him, making him uncomfortable.

"Stop looking at me," Catfish warned and, pulling his gun out again, fired at Michael.

This time the bullet hit her in the right shoulder. It took her to the ground.

She didn't fight when he pulled her to her feet and dragged her to the chaise lounge. He stretched her out and sat over her so he could look down into her face.

"It's time to finish this. I need to get back to my wife and kids. My anniversary is in two days, and I promised my lovely wife we would go on a cruise. Sounds fun, doesn't it?" Catfish continued as he ran his hand down her neck, over her breast, and allowed it to travel toward the lacy top of her panties.

His attention was focused on her breasts, one hand unsnapping the front hook that would release the thin material and free her, the other hand caressing his erection.

The blow landed hard against his left temple. Whatever she had concealed in her hand was hard enough to send him to the ground. Catfish felt the warmth of blood trickle down his face.

"That, Michael, will be the last thing that you ever do," Catfish said as he got to his feet, pulling the cord out of his pocket. He stood over her, looking into her eyes. They were filled, not with fear, but defiance, seeing that defiance enraged him.

He pulled the length of the clothesline tight and wrapped the cord around her neck. Before he began pulling it, Catfish leaned over so his face was inches from hers. "All I wanted was you to love me like I loved you," he finally confessed.

Michael slapped and punched at him as he pulled the cord tighter and tighter, but it didn't matter. In the end, he was stronger.

CHAPTER 45

Dan, Carson, and several uniformed officers reached the roof while the EMT waited in the stairwell. As they reached the scene, each yelled at the attacker to stop and step away from the body that had ceased to struggle seconds after they arrived.

Dan heard the shot but didn't know who had fired it. The man over Michael, strangling her, turned and looked at the four of them. Then he smiled and looked at Dan. "You're too late, the Abomination is gone."

His body hit the cobblestone surface of the roof with a thud.

CHAPTER 46

Michael became aware of voices. They were faint, not real. Pain began to make its presence known. It was subtle, but as the voices became clearer, the pain became more focused.

Light seeped under Michael's eyelids, burning through. The light added to the pain.

Michael tried to move.

"Michael," a familiar voice in Michael's left ear said.

"Michael," another voice spoke, "if you can understand me, squeeze your left hand."

Michael concentrated on squeezing but wasn't sure if the connection from hand to brain was working.

"She's responding," the voice, a third, said.

"Michael, just relax. We're going to get you stabilized here and get you to the hospital," a voice told her.

"Michael," the first voice said, and she recognized it as Dan's. "Michael, don't you die on me. I've waited all my life for you."

Michael willed her arm to move in the direction of Dan's voice.

"No," the other voice warned, "don't move. Officer Hartman is going to go with you to the hospital, so don't worry."

"Michael, honey, I'm sorry," Dan's disembodied voice said. The words registered in her foggy brain, but it was the light touch of lips on hers that really connected. It was the last thing Michael understood before she faded back into unconsciousness.

CHAPTER 47

The smell was familiar. Michael was in the hospital. She could hear movement around her and feel someone holding her hand. She opened her eyes and raised the hand that wasn't being held. She discovered the diamond engagement ring placed on her finger.

Michael turned to see who had possession of her hand. Although it was only the top of his head, Michael knew it was Dan. She ran her fingers through his thick black hair and watched as he lifted his head.

"Michael," he said her name as if whispering a prayer. It held so much meaning and emotion; Michael was breathless.

She looked around and saw Sean and David sitting on the sofa, their attention focused on her. In unison they stood and headed toward the bed.

"Hey, sister," Sean said as he leaned over to kiss her, "I've been worried about you."

"You really know how to keep the men in your life on edge, don't you?" David said before adding, "Come on, Sean, let's go get some coffee."

Michael watched as David reached over and touched his brother's hand. She felt the silent communication between the twins before David, with Sean in tow, left.

Her attention shifted from the backs of the two men to Dan's face.

"Michael, I need you to forgive me." His voice was filled with the tears that were unshed in his brown eyes. "I'm a fucking idiot, you should know that. It was just that all this was such a surprise. I know you tried to tell me, and I didn't listen." Dan moved from the chair to the hospital bed. He took her in his arms. Kissing her before continuing, "I love you. I don't care about your past or what you were twenty-five years ago. All I know is you are the woman I want to spend the rest of my life with. If you let me, I will spend the next one hundred years showing you how much I love you and how sorry I am for saying those terrible things to you."

Michael held up her hand to silence him. She understood how it must have been for him, finding out about her that way. Michael could only imagine how emotionally unsettling it must be to discover what she had been through in her life.

She knew Dan meant what he told her.

Michael didn't sign anything but simply pulled Dan to her and kissed him as if her very soul depended on his kiss to survive.

It did!

EPILOGUE

Michael had returned to the condo on Stanford Street after five days in the hospital. Dan had been placed on administrative leave, pending the outcome of the investigation, as there had been a firearm used and an individual shot and killed. Even though Dan had not pulled the trigger, all four of the police officers who had been on the roof had been put on leave.

Michael's mother and grandmother had flown in from Ireland to help with Michael's recovery and to be supportive of their children. At Michael's suggestion, Dan and David's parents had flown in from DC to lend the same support as well.

The media firestorm started the sixth day after Michael had been shot.

The local television stations and newspaper ran the story the night of the shooting. A local woman, they had said, was attacked and shot in her downtown loft. The Houston Police Department had responded to a phone call and had caught the attacker as he was attempting to strangle the woman. The attacker, a Georgian man named Kenneth Morris, was shot and killed by police.

If that had been it, the only reports about the situation, there would have been no problems. There would have been no exploitation of their lives on the nation's airwaves.

Michael glanced down at the latest copy of the *Houston Chronicle* and shook her head. She had to give the reporter credit for doing his job, but he had done it too well. First he came across the information that Kenneth Morris was the uncle, half-brother of Michael's father.

Then, after digging further, he connected Sean. Kenneth Morris, Michael Braun, and Sean Fitzpatrick were really Kenneth Branson Mosby, Michael Hannah Mosby, and Sean Dean Mosby. Michael and Sean had known that with this information, the article for the *British Journal of Medicine* and the rest of the family history wouldn't be far behind. It hadn't taken long.

It was with the last bit of information that their lives had become open to the world. All four major networks carried the story as well as CNN and, because of Sean, ESPN.

For Michael, the media feeding frenzy was only half as bad as it was for Sean, Dan, and David. Because David and Kelly were out as a gay couple and were respected members of both the medical and gay communities in Houston, they were protected by their friends, colleagues, and the communities they were part of.

Sean had been grilled but not roasted in the media. After asking permission from his sister and Dan, Sean had agreed to an exclusive interview by ESPN's top sports reporter. He had explained the situation with his uncle and his twisted obsession with his sister, Michael. It was after this show that the three major companies that used Sean as a spokesman announced publicly they intended to keep Sean on and praised his devotion to his family. The only drawback, Sean had confessed to Michael, was that he had become the unofficial poster boy for the gay, lesbian, and transgender community, something he had no desire to be. However, he admitted the reason he hadn't lost any contracts was because the companies were hoping to reap the benefits of his unexpected association with that community.

Dan, unfortunately, caught the majority of the fallout. Luckily for him, most of the men and woman he worked with didn't care about his personal life and supported and protected him from the media. Carson, Garcia, Parker, and Danton had all been approached to give interviews about the local police detective and his "friend." They all refused, with the exception of Captain Parker, who gave a prepared statement to the press, informing them of Dan's, Detective Hartman's, outstanding service record for the City of Houston, Harris, Fort Bend, Galveston, and Brazoria County's law enforcement departments and encouraging the press to respect his privacy and that of his fellow officers.

Michael had agreed to speak with the *Houston Chronicle* reporter who had dug up all the information on her and those she loved. With an interpreter's help, Michael answered all his questions. She had been surprised at his thoroughness in his research and his interview. Michael withheld nothing, with the exception of her physical relationship with Dan. The reporter had pushed, only once, but agreed that what Michael and Dan did in their bedroom was their business after Michael had told the reporter she would tell him everything after she had had the opportunity to discuss his sex life with his wife of fifteen years. He had smiled and gone on.

She admitted she hadn't told Dan about her background although had intended to. Michael did everything in her power to draw the attention off Dan and onto her.

Before the article went to print for the weekend edition, she had the unusual privilege of viewing the article. The reporter had wanted to assure Michael he had been fair to her as well as Dan. Michael had been impressed at the human angle of the article. It showed them as a man and woman in a loving relationship, caught in an extremely extraordinary situation. She had thanked him and told him if there was a wedding, he and his wife would get invitations.

Now two weeks had passed, and although it was old news, it was still news. Sean had told her only this morning, his life was getting closer to what it had been, to what he considered normal. Both her Irish family and Dan and David's parents had returned home, having helped their children weather the storm.

Dan, as well as Carson and the other two officers, had been put back on regular assignment as of that morning.

Michael had waited all day long to hear from Dan. She hadn't been surprised he hadn't texted her. She knew he was going to be busy, trying to get into the swing of things but still she waited.

Their relationship hadn't changed. After Dan had spent the first few days apologizing and admitting to being an idiot, Michael had convinced him she had forgiven him. They had spent the following week trying to get through each day as it happened. At night they held each other, and it was then they felt safe from the judgments and prejudices of the outside world that seemed to want to tear them apart.

Michael heard the garage door open then close. She had made a light dinner, not knowing how hungry Dan would be or how much either would be able to eat. She stood in the kitchen and waited.

When Dan walked through the door, Michael let out a sigh of relief. He had a smile on his face and a dozen roses in his hand.

Michael walked forward, wrapping her arms around him, mouthing the words, "For me?"

Dan kissed her, and she turned to liquid fire before stepping away. "They are for you but not from me. Captain Parker told me to tell you to take good care of your future husband. This was his idea of a bribe and a thank-you. I'm not sure for what. I didn't ask."

Michael took the flowers and took a moment to put them in a vase.

"Dan," Michael started but stopped.

"Michael," Dan interrupted her, "this is all going to work out. Do you know how I know?"

She shook her head. She hadn't a clue.

He took her hand and began to lead her upstairs. Michael stopped at the foot of the stairs.

Dan looked at her, questioningly.

"I know because I know what would have happened to me if I had lost you. I know because if you weren't in my life, I don't think I'd feel alive. Before you, I just went through the motions of life. You breathed life into me, you fired my soul." He resumed his ascent up the stairs with her behind him.

Michael thought to herself as Dan began to kiss her neck, his fingers working the buttons of her jeans, that she knew exactly what Dan had meant.

Dan had engulfed Michael in his love, surprised her, and opened her up to what she had been missing in her life.

Maybe it wouldn't last.

But maybe, just maybe, it would.